GHOST
A Lords of Carnage MC Romance

DAPHNE LOVELING

Copyright © 2017 Daphne Loveling

All rights reserved.
ISBN-13:
978-1544240916

ISBN-10:
1544240910

This book is a work of fiction.

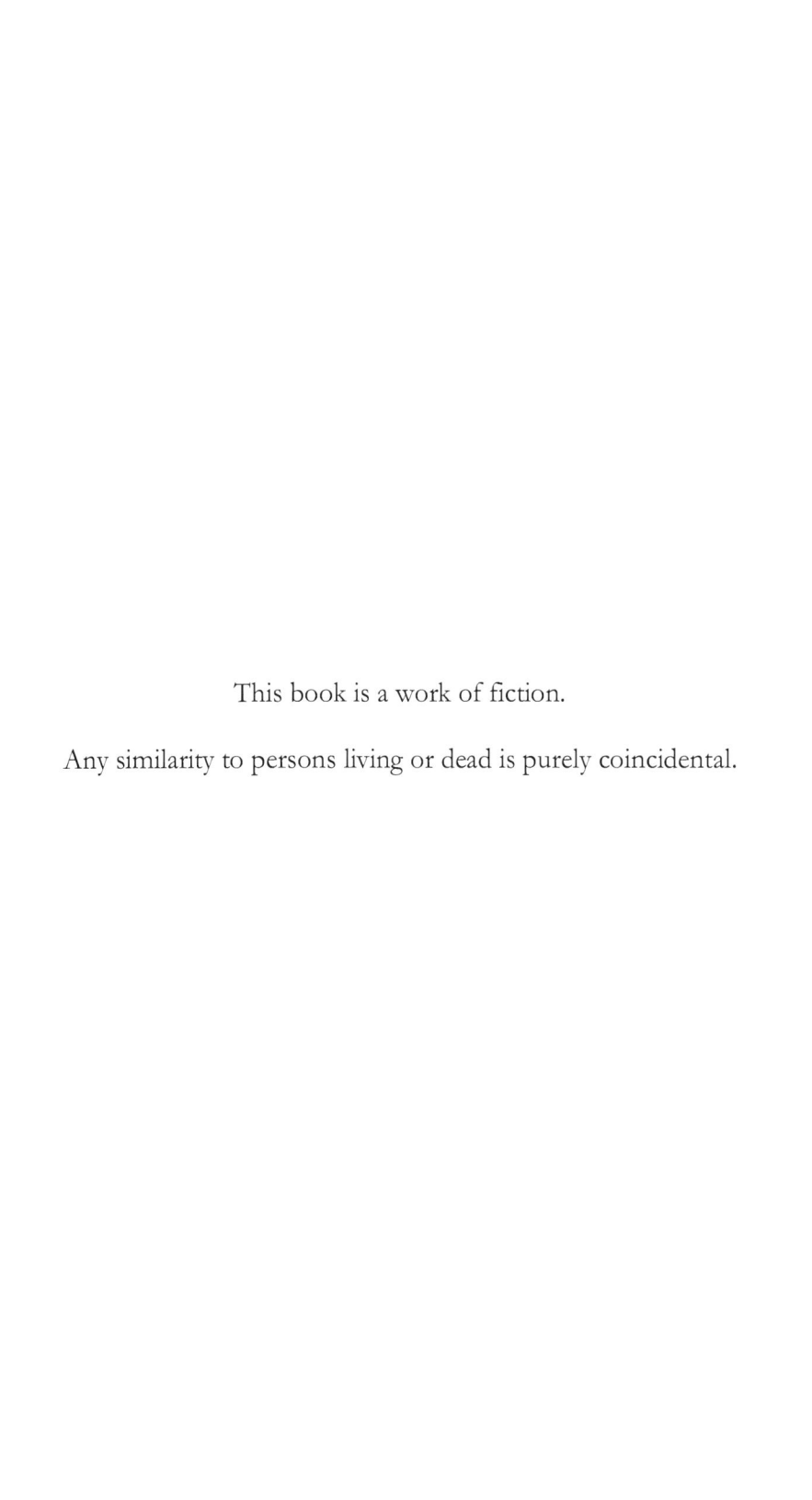

Any similarity to persons living or dead is purely coincidental.

To my readers.

May you always remember: it's better to regret something you have done than something you haven't done.

Chapter 1

JENNA

Mistakes.

Sometimes it seems like my entire life has been one long one.

Sometimes you rack up so many of them, you can't work out where one mistake ends and the next one begins.

That's how it feels right now, returning to Tanner Springs. The site of most of my biggest mistakes.

Once, it was home.

Then, it was anything but.

And now, I'm back. And I don't know if it can ever be anything like home again.

* * *

"Oof," Angel grunts as he drops the last of the boxes onto the old moth-eaten sofa. It's a big, heavy paper ream box full of books — one of a few I've been lugging around from place to place for the last few years. Old college textbooks, mostly. The remnants of a dream I should have given up on by now.

"Is that the last one, I hope?" he says. It's pretty evident by the look on his face what he hopes my answer is.

"Yeah, that's it," I nod, and resist the urge to apologize. Even though he offered to help me move in to my new apartment, I still feel guilty accepting the favor.

I watch my brother pull up the front of his black T-shirt, revealing a snarl of tattoos on his stomach and chest. He wipes the sweat from his face with the fabric, then pulls it back down. "You want something to drink?" I ask him. "I think I can find the box of glasses in the kitchen."

"You got any beer? I sure could use one." He raises his arms out in a massive stretch.

"Sorry, no," I say regretfully. "I haven't had time to go shopping yet." One more thing on my mental list of things to do, I remind myself. There's no food in the house, either, and it's getting close to supper time. I'll need to find something for Noah and me to eat.

I heave an exhausted sigh at the thought of trying to make a grocery run with a wound-up and hungry four-year-old. *Hell.* Maybe I'll just give in and order a pizza, I reason. I can take care of the grocery shopping tomorrow, when I've had a good night's sleep.

Speaking of the wound-up four-year-old, my son Noah emerges from what will be his new bedroom. His arms are out in a T and he's making a buzzing noise with his lips as though he's a prop plane. He "flies" around the room, circling the boxes and crates, then crashes into Angel's legs as he turns toward the kitchen.

"Hey, easy, buddy," Angel said, looking slightly annoyed. "Look, go play somewhere else, okay?" Angel shoots me a glance. "He sure is keyed up."

"He's been cooped up all day," I explain, again resisting the urge to apologize. "First in the U-Haul and now in here. He's bored."

Noah flies back down the hall toward his room. I know my brother doesn't have a lot of experience with kids, so he probably doesn't realize how easily they get antsy. Actually, I've been pretty impressed at how little Noah's been acting out today, given the circumstances. "He's only four," I tell Angel. "He doesn't have great impulse control."

I wander the few steps into the kitchen and look around for the box labeled "glassware." Pulling off the tape, I grab one of Noah's plastic glasses with a picture of Thomas the Tank Engine out of the box. I turn to the sink and hold it under the faucet. Water sputters violently when I twist the

3

handle, and I start and take a quick step back. Brownish liquid begins to run out of the tap.

"This apartment hasn't been used in a while, the landlord said." Angel comes up behind me and peers at the dubious-looking water. "You probably want to run that for a few minutes."

As I wait for the water to turn clear, I look around me at the dingy tile floor and dusty, grease-tacky counter tops. This entire place needs a good scrubbing from top to bottom. Still, I have no business complaining. Noah and I are lucky to have a roof over our heads at all, given everything that's happened in the last few months. It isn't paradise, but it's home for now. More importantly, it's all I can afford.

"Thanks for helping me, Angel," I murmur. "Moving all these boxes up a flight of stairs wouldn't have been easy with just me and Noah." I fill up the glass with now clearish water and hand it to him.

Angel takes the glass and frowns at it. "No worries," he shrugs, then takes a long drink of water, his Adam's apple moving as he gulps it down. When he's finished, he sets the glass on the counter and wipes his mouth with the back of his hand. "You sure you don't want to tell me what happened back in the city, to make you come back to Tanner Springs?" he asks, eyeing me curiously.

I take in a deep breath and let it out. "Yeah," I say. "I'm sure."

I don't want to talk about it. Just more mistakes, more bad choices. This one involved taking a job at a place I shouldn't have, even though my warning bells were going off the second I noticed the boss's eyes roving over me during the interview. When he tried putting his paws all over me one night after hours, I fought back, and he fired my ass on the spot. Not only that, he stiffed me out of my final paycheck, knowing it would take a lawyer I couldn't afford to get it back from him. A couple months later, I was late on my rent one too many times, and got evicted. What kind of heartless asshole evicts a single mother with a four-year-old child?

My shoulders sag with fatigue just thinking about it all. I'm so tired of looking back at the past and regretting things. I want a fresh start, eyes pointed toward the future. And I'm determined to have that fresh start, too. Even if it has to happen here, in a place that's full of all sorts of memories both bad and good.

Angel sighs. "Okay. No skin off my nose." He glances toward an ancient-looking, yellowed phone sitting on a ledge between the kitchen and the living room. "By the way, Jenna, Dad wants you to call him when you get settled in. He left his phone number over there in case you needed it."

Somehow, I hadn't noticed the phone at all when we'd been moving boxes and furniture in. "Oh, my gosh, is that a *land* line?" I say in disbelief. "I haven't seen one of these things in a house in years."

"Yeah," Angel laughs. "I tried it. It even works." He picks up the receiver and holds it out to me so I can hear the drone of the dial tone. I look closer. Wow. It's even a rotary phone, not a push-button one.

I shake my head and laugh. "That's so weird. I wonder if the last person to live here just forgot to shut it off?" I won't look a gift horse in the mouth, though. My cell phone service is pretty basic, so being able to make some local calls from home without wasting my minutes will be kind of nice.

I pick up the stickie note that's been stuck next to the phone. On it, in my dad's unmistakable handwriting, are the words: "Jenna. Call me as soon as you're able. Dad." The phone number for his office is scrawled underneath. I make a mental note to call my dad and thank him for setting me up with a place to live. As much as I hate to be in anybody's debt, it's only fair that I express my gratitude.

Though, by rights, I'm not really sure whether I owe the cheap apartment find to him, or to the Lords of Carnage.

And I don't know which debt would be worse.

Chapter 2
JENNA

The Lords of Carnage is the local motorcycle club in Tanner Springs. It basically runs this town, and what it doesn't directly run, it controls by influence — through protection deals it has with local businesses, or connections under the table with the local city government.

My father is the mayor of Tanner Springs. Has been for years, in fact. Since I was a little girl. He's also cozy as hell with the Lords of Carnage. The motorcycle club helped him get elected to the position all those years ago. I'm not sure what kind of a deal my father struck with the MC back then, but he's reciprocated their support by doing them all manner of favors ever since. The full nature and scope of these favors, I don't know, and I don't want to know. But I do know he and the MC are tight. Tighter than an outlaw biker club probably should be with the mayor of their town. But then, that's none of my business.

The relationship between my dad and the club has only gotten tighter in recent years, too. Ever since my brother Gabriel decided to prospect for the Lords when he turned eighteen. Since getting patched in to the club, he's been known around town by his road name: Angel. In the six years that he's been in the club, my brother has quickly risen up through their ranks, and now, he's their vice-president.

All of this means that, between my dad and my brother, there is almost no way for me to stay away from the Lords of Carnage when I'm in Tanner Springs. This tiny two-bedroom apartment where Noah and I will be staying for the foreseeable future is in the top floor of a house right off Main Street. The floor below houses the tattoo parlor that the Lords of Carnage frequents. So, I don't really know whether the club or my dad got this place for me. But I'm guessing that the landlord, who lives in the house next door and whose name is Charlie, was only too happy to do a solid for the club and the mayor at the same time.

Whether my father or the MC found the place for me, though, I hate like hell to be indebted to either of them. My father's political ambitions have always taken precedent over his family's needs, and I'm used to being ignored unless he needs something from me. His favors always come with a price. And as for the club… well, they've been a presence in my life almost from the moment I was born. They're pretty much inescapable. They own this town, and so to some extent, they own practically everyone in it.

I left Tanner Springs in part because I didn't want them to own me, as well. Unfortunately, my life circumstances are such at the moment that I have little choice but to move back here temporarily and accept the help they've offered — if, in fact, they've offered it. But as soon as I'm back on my feet, my intention is to get myself and my son the hell away from here.

After this, I don't want to be in anyone's debt, ever again.

I open my mouth to tell Angel I'll call Dad later, when a noise from down the hall interrupts me. With a yell that sounds like a high-pitched war whoop, Noah comes barreling back into the living room, flying over the arm of the ratty couch and doing a somersault onto the cushions.

"Mom mom mom mom mom!" he cries. "I'm hungry!"

I shush him. "Okay, honey. Calm down. We'll eat soon."

Noah jumps up from the couch and starts running in circles around Angel. "Moommm!" he yells again, "I'm HUNGRY!"

"Noah, stop it," I admonish. "Indoor voice."

"Okay, I'm out," Angel calls above the din. Clearly, he's had enough four-year-old for one day. "See you later, sis."

Noah immediately quiets. "Are you leaving, Uncle Angel?"

"Yeah, buddy, I'm taking off." Angel grabs his leather cut from where it's hanging on one of the kitchen chairs.

"Can I have a ride on your motorcycle?" Noah asks, his eyes big as saucers.

"Sorry, bud, you're a little too young yet." Angel reaches out and ruffles my son's dark brown hair. "One of these days, though, maybe."

Angel turns and clomps out of the apartment, his heavy motorcycle boots thumping loudly as he descends to the first floor. A few seconds later, the rumble of Angel's motorcycle below reaches us. Noah immediately runs to the window and stares in fascination as the bike drives off, his nose pressed hard against the glass.

I watch my son and try to push down the spike of worry that rises up inside me. Noah has always been transfixed by motorcycles. He's had a near-obsession with the machines almost from his birth. As I stand there contemplating my young son, I hope like hell I'm not making yet another huge mistake by bringing him here to Tanner Springs. I'd hate to look back at this moment as a possible reason he ended up getting mixed up with a damn motorcycle club — like every other member of my family seems to in one way or another.

Including Noah's father.

I shake my head and take a deep breath, letting it out slowly. I just have to hope that love of two-wheeled vehicles isn't something that's passed down genetically. Noah has no idea who his father is, and Noah's dad has no idea he has a son.

And I've been telling myself for years that everyone is better off that way. If I could manage to keep it a secret, I reasoned, Noah would grow up not knowing that father is an outlaw biker. And the man who knocked me up almost five years ago will never have to know that our brief, meaningless fling produced anything more than an earth-shattering orgasm and a wave of regret the next morning.

Not that I could ever regret having my son. Noah is the only good thing that's ever come out of one of my multitude of mistakes. Sure, being a single mom has been tough. There have been times when I wasn't quite sure how I would ever make it through. But even so, I wouldn't trade being Noah's mom for anything. My little boy is sweet, sensitive, and the center of my world. Not to mention smart as a whip. Too smart, sometimes. At age four, he's already reading, and I sometimes wonder how long I have before he knows more than his mama does.

About six months ago, when we were still in Denver, he started to realize that most of his little playmates had a mommy and a daddy. Not long after, he began asking me where his father was, who he was, why he didn't live with us. Noah is clearly starting to look for male role models to emulate. Which is why I'm not exactly thrilled to see him staring out the window in longing as Angel drives away on his bike. I love my brother, but he isn't exactly my idea of the man I want Noah to model himself after.

Little does my son know that his own father is a biker, as well. But I can't imagine that Noah's dad would react with anything other than dismay if I told him that he had procreated. And there's no way I'm going to saddle my son with a father who's indifferent to him. It's better for him to have no father at all than a father like that. At least, that's what I tell myself.

So, I've kept my secrets buried deep inside me. I've reconciled myself to the fact that Noah will probably grow up not ever knowing his dad. Although recent events, and moving back here to my hometown, might make that a little more complicated.

As I watch my young son stare out the window watching his uncle drive away, I make myself a solemn promise then and there. Even though I'm back in Tanner Springs — site of some of my stupidest mistakes — I'm done doing dumb things that will come back to haunt me. Today marks the end of the past, I tell myself. No more dwelling on things that have already happened. No regrets. But no more mistakes, either.

Chapter 3

CAS

The best thing about being away from Tanner Springs? Coming home.

I roll up to the clubhouse to a raucous welcome from my brothers. I've been gone for about three weeks, on some club business for the MC. The club president, Rocco Anthony, sent me out on some business for him as Sergeant at Arms for the Lords of Carnage. I was traveling around to some other chapters to deliver some confidential information in person. I have no issue doing whatever the prez asks me to — hell, just the chance to spend some hours on the open road means I'm always up for a trip — but damn, it feels good to get back to my town and hang out with my club.

My return is timed to correspond with a club meeting that is supposed to happen later this afternoon, which Rock specifically wants me to be at. Apparently some shit's gone down while I was away. But luckily, there's still time before church to throw back a few shots and accept the back slaps of the other men as they welcome me home.

Jewel, a sandy-haired, buxom bartender with killer legs, pours a line of shots down the bar for me and my brothers. Gunner, Shifter, and Tank hold theirs up to me, and the four of us pound them back. Then we set them down for Jewel to serve us another round. I shoot the shit with the men for a few minutes, but eventually I find myself scanning the room for my best buddy, Angel. I finally see him back by the pool table, talking to a couple of the other brothers, one hand absently sliding up the skirt of one of the club girls.

Detaching myself from the men, I amble over to where Angel is and slap him on the back. "Hey, fucker," I say.

"My man Ghost!" Angel yells with a wide grin. "Long time no fuckin' see!" He's clearly started drinking before me, and is feeling no pain. "All right, y'all, I gotta go catch up with my brother." He holds up the bottle he's been drinking from and turns to me. "Grab a beer and come outside to have a smoke with me, man."

Ghost is my road name. Since my parents named me Casper, I supposed you'd think the choice was a gimme. But that's not the main reason they call me that. They call me Ghost because I wait. I stay silent and in the shadows, watching and biding my time. I don't make my move until

I'm absolutely sure of everything. If I'm coming for you, you'll never even know I'm there. Until it's too late.

I signal to Jewel at the bar and she nods and opens a cold bottle of beer for me, then hands it to me as I walk by. Outside, Angel lights up a smoke and offers me one, which I take. He leans against the outer wall of the clubhouse and cocks his head at me.

"So, fucker, what's been goin' on? How's the pussy up north?"

I laugh. "About the same as the pussy down here. A little colder." I take a pull of my beer and nod toward the inside of the clubhouse. "You got any idea what this meeting's about? Rock said it was important, but he didn't tell me much more. Just that I needed to get down here for it."

"Yeah, I got some idea," Angel replies vaguely. "But best wait for you to hear it from the prez. Too much to explain, and fuck it, we're not on the clock yet." He raises the smoke to his lips and takes a long drag, then blows it out. "Hey, you know, you ain't the only one back in town. Guess who showed up a couple days ago?"

"Who's that?" I have no idea who he could be talking about.

"My little sis." He takes another puff. "Seems Jenna got her fool self evicted from her place in the city. Lost her job to boot. She's moving back here for a bit. To get back on her feet, she says." Angel spits. "That girl is one goddamn hot mess."

I freeze, my bottle lifted halfway to my lips. "Jenna's back in town?"

Shit. I haven't seen Jenna Abbott for what, almost five years? She hardly ever gets back to Tanner Springs. The last time I can remember was when she flunked out of college one semester, and came back here for a few months until she scraped together enough money to leave again. I remember it well. Hell, it would be hard to forget, after what happened between us the night before she left. I still think about it from time to time, on the rare occasions that I spend the night alone.

"Yeah," Angel shrugs. "She's back. Dad set her and her kid up in the apartment above Rebel Ink."

"Her kid?" I blink in surprise. I don't remember Angel or their dad Abe mentioning that Jenna had a kid. Then again, they almost never talk about Jenna at all.

"Yup. A boy. Noah, his name is." Angel throws his butt on the ground, not bothering to grind it out with his heel. "He's what, four? I think that's what she said." He snorts and shakes his head. "I helped Jenna move in, and the kid wouldn't stop screamin' and tear-assin' around. I don't even know why the hell people have kids anyway."

"If no one had kids, you wouldn't be here," I point out absently. Angel changes the subject then, and starts talking about the new tattoo he got while I was gone, but I tune him out.

Holy hell. Jenna Abbott.

My mind flashes on an image of her, as clear and fresh as the last time I saw her. She's a girl who makes an impression. Light, almost transparent blue eyes that you could almost drown in, like clear water. Thick, wavy blond hair that other women notice and comment on when she walks by, and that makes a man want to fist his hands in. Full, plump lips that have always reminded me of ripe, fleshy fruit. They made me want to taste them every time I looked at them, long before I actually did.

Fuck. Big mistake letting myself think about Jenna. Before I can do anything to stop it, my dick is instantly hard. Hoping like hell Angel won't notice anything, I quickly sit down on a stack of old tires a couple feet away and pretend I'm listening to him, nodding my head so he won't notice I'm tuning him out.

I've known Jenna Abbott for practically my whole life. At least a dozen years now. The first time I met her, she was just a kid, but on the cusp of puberty. So I had a front row seat to her entire transformation from girl to woman. At the time, of course, I was going through my own adolescence, so I got to watch her grow tits and hips just as my hormones began to rage out of control.

She was one of my guiltiest fantasies when I would jack off at night in my darkened bedroom. The next day, I'd see

Angel (he went by his real name, Gabe, back then) and I'd wonder if he could see it in my face that I was beating my meat to thoughts of my best friend's sister. Of course, looking back on it now, I'm sure he never suspected a thing. It was just my guilty conscience bothering me. Thankfully, it's not like Gabe and I spent a lot of time around her, anyway. Still, I saw her just often enough around school and town for her to be one of the rotating mental images in my spank bank.

By the time we were in high school, I discovered that most of the girls in my class were more than willing to get down and dirty with me in the back of any car I could beg, borrow or steal. Little by little, I forgot about Jenna Abbott's hot little body through the distraction of all the easy tail I was getting. Eventually, I graduated high school (barely), and the next I heard, Jenna had gone off to college.

My adolescent obsession with her probably would have ended right there, relegated to a mere footnote in my sexual history. That is, if she hadn't moved back to Tanner Springs after flunking out of college at the end of her freshman year.

What happened between us that summer was something no one but the two of us ever knew about. I sure as hell wasn't going to tell her brother, or even worse, her father. It had been just a fling, anyway. Just a summer hookup between two people whose bodies didn't seem to be able to get enough of each other. I shift uncomfortably on the stack of tires now as my dick grows even harder at the memory. Even with all the women I've had — far too many to count by now

— Jenna Abbott stands out as the hottest, most fuckable piece of ass I've ever had the pleasure of sinking my cock into.

And now she's back in town again.

Probably not good.

Striker opens the back door to the club and sticks his head out. "Hey. Rock says church in five."

Angel straightens. "Got it." Turning to me, he asked, "You ready?"

"Yeah," I reply, nodding over toward the bushes. "Just gotta take a leak first."

Angel follows Striker inside, and I stand and head off to talk my dick down and take piss.

So Jenna has a kid now. Damn. It's hard to imagine; she's still so young, maybe twenty-three or twenty-four now. I wonder what kind of curve ball life threw at her to make her a mom — though I imagine she'd probably be a good one, despite Angel's griping about the kid. Angel isn't exactly known for his patience.

Heading back inside for church, I find myself wondering how long Jenna's going to stay in Tanner Springs this time. It's gonna be tough to stay away from her, since now I know from our fling last time she was in town what she's like in the sack. What *we* were like together. Sex with Jenna was off the goddamn charts. But that shit was dangerous back then, and nothing makes it any less dangerous now. Jenna Abbott needs to be off limits, I tell myself. Period.

I wander into the chapel after most of the guys are already there. As I take my place at the table, I get my first good look at most of the brothers since I got back. To my surprise, I see some fresh bruises I didn't notice before in the dark of the bar. The expressions on their faces are tense, jaws set in tight grimaces. I realize now why Rock told me to be back for today's meeting.

Looks like some shit has gone down while I was away.

Chapter 4
JENNA

The stickie note with my dad's office number and the request that I call him is still sitting next to the land line phone the next day. I glance at it guiltily as I clear Noah's lunch of canned spaghetti and meatballs — one of the only things I can get him to eat at the moment. Noah's been restless for most of the morning, clamoring for me to take him to the park he noticed a few blocks away when we first drove through town. But the park is going to have to wait a bit. First, I need to spend some time hunting for a job.

I put Noah's bowl in the sink and slouch down on the old, saggy sofa with my laptop. Immediately, Noah comes to sit down beside me, a wad of blue Play-Doh in his hand. "Look, Mommy, a dinosaur!" he beseeches, holding up a blob that could just as soon be a bunny rabbit. Or a cantaloupe, for that matter.

"Nice, bug," I smile at him and log into a local job search site.

"Wait, wait! How about this? Mommy, can you tell what this is?" I look over again to see he has ever-so-slightly modified the blob by sticking another blob on top of it.

"Hmmm, I'm not sure," I frown. "Is it... a fire engine?"

"No!" he says crossly, genuinely disappointed at my lack of vision. "It's Sponge Bob!"

I suppress a sigh, realizing that the "guess what this is" game is probably going to go on forever unless I do something to stop it. "Bug, I have an idea," I say, sitting up and putting the laptop on the coffee table in front of me. "How about you watch some Paw Patrol? Mommy's got a little work to do."

"Okay!" Noah says happily. He is *always* up for Paw Patrol. I find some episodes for him on YouTube. Then, when he's situated and quiet, I pull my cell phone out of my pocket and head into the bedroom to resume my job search that way.

Just as I sit down on my unmade bed to start looking, the phone rings in my hand, startling me. It's my father, calling from his personal number. I suppress a groan and answer.

"Hey, Dad," I say.

"Jenna!" his voice booms through the phone. "You haven't called me yet."

I purse my lips against his admonishment. "Well, we're talking now," I say, keeping my voice bright. "What's up?"

"Checking in on my daughter," he says gruffly. "You all moved in?"

"Yes," I tell him, and lean back against a pillow. "Not unpacked, but everything's in the apartment. By the way, I wanted to thank you for helping me out with finding this place."

"Well, it sure ain't much of an apartment, that's for sure," he huffs. "But with the budget you gave me there weren't many options. I don't know why you don't just move into the house. God knows there's enough room for the two of you there."

"Thanks, Dad, but no." It had been hard enough for me to ask my father's help in finding the apartment. If there's one thing I know about Dad from long experience, it's that Abe "Triple A" Abbott's help always comes with strings attached. He's a born politician, and like all politicians, the main currency he deals in is favors. And the favors he demands in exchange for his help are too rich for my blood.

It is true, though, that there would be more than enough space for Noah and me at Dad's place. Even though my mom has been dead for years, he's still rattling around by himself in the house I grew up in. I've never been quite sure why, when it seems like he'd probably be much more comfortable in a smaller place. He has to hire a service to mow his lawn, and another service to clean his house. He works so much that he's hardly ever home, anyway. It's baffling. But maybe it's just his pride as the mayor of Tanner Springs that keeps him from downsizing to a condo or something.

Dad's still rambling on about how much more sense it would make for me to move back home with him for a while, like he hasn't heard me refuse a dozen times already. I'm trying to think of a way to wind down the conversation gracefully, but apparently he's not through grilling me. "You found yourself a job yet?" he barks. In the background, I can hear a door slam.

I roll my eyes. "Dad, I just got here yesterday. I was just going to start looking through some ads when you called."

"You know, I'm sure if I asked around, we could find you something right quick," he offers. "Probably better pay than you're used to, too."

I decide to ignore the dig, in part because it's true. "No thanks, Dad." The last thing I want is to be making some artificially bloated salary on some local business owner's payroll just because I'm the mayor's daughter. Whatever job I end up finding — even if it's a crappy one — I want it to be on my own merits, however small they are.

Desperate to change the subject away from my considerable shortcomings, I turn the conversation to the one thing I know will distract him from grilling me about my future. "So, Dad, how's the reelection campaign going?" I ask.

"Oh, Jesus Christ," he spits out in a disgusted voice. I hear him grunt as he heaves his hefty body into a chair. "That fuckin' Holloway is gonna be the death of me. That little piss-ant came back to Tanner Springs after college with a two-bit MBA and a two-by-four stuck so far up his ass it's tickling his tonsils."

I know already that my father is worried that his challenger, Jarred Holloway, is pulling ahead of him in the mayoral race. Holloway's younger, hungry for power, and good-looking in a frat bro kind of way. According to Angel, he's making his campaign about Tanner Springs needing "New Blood, and New Ideas." It's even on his campaign signs, which I've already seen scattered throughout the town. Dad's taking it as a personal affront, and it's kind of consuming him.

"That underhanded son of a bitch is spreading all sorts of bullshit about me to anyone who'll listen," Dad's ranting. To me, it sounds like maybe Holloway has learned a few things from my dad's playbook and is threatening to beat him at his own game. "What in the hell has that arrogant pile of shit ever done for this goddamn town? These people are a bunch'a ungrateful sons of bitches. I have sacrificed everything for this town. *Everything*, do you hear me?"

His voice is rising now, and I imagine that his secretary and other employees can hear him on the other side of his office door. "Dad, calm down," I soothe.

"Calm down? How the hell am I gonna calm down when that fuckin' wolf is breathing down my neck?"

"I don't know, Dad," I sigh. "But I'm pretty sure you aren't doing yourself any good letting yourself get worked up like this."

Well, I got him to change the subject away from me, all right. But if anything this one's almost worse. I try again to steer the conversation to something a little more neutral before he works himself up into a heart attack.

"Hey, Dad, I was wondering if you know anything about which are the good preschools in the area." I want to get Noah enrolled in something soon, for some socialization with other kids his age. I'm hoping Dad will bite, and he does. Abe Abbott loves to be asked for advice, even if it's on a subject he knows absolutely nothing about. His tone changes from angry to authoritative in an instant as he begins to rattle off names of different places in the area. For each one, he interjects comments about whether their directors have supported him or not during his mayoral campaigns. I listen with half an ear as I absently finger the ring I wear on a chain around my neck.

"Of course, I don't think you can afford that one," he says as continues to editorialize about one of the preschools he's heard good things about. "It's probably the best preschool in town, and it ain't cheap. Not a lot of bartenders' or waitresses' kids going there."

His bluntness probably isn't meant to be cruel, but it sure feels that way. My breath hitches a little at his words, and he must hear it, because his tone instantly softens.

"I'm sorry, Jenna. I didn't mean it to sound that way. I guess I just wish you'd finished college, is all," he says, sounding momentarily subdued. "Maybe if you had you wouldn't be in the 'situation' you're in right now."

"That makes two of us, Daddy," I murmur under my breath. I know he means well. But sometimes I wonder if his concern about me not finishing college has more to do with feeling that a mayor's daughter shouldn't be slinging drinks at a bar.

"Well," he says abruptly, his voice returning to the rapid-fire bark I know so well. "You let me know if you need me to find you something. And come by the house this weekend. Bring your boy with you. It's not right that I haven't seen my grandson yet."

"I will," I promise him, even though I know from experience that he'll spend about a minute fussing over Noah before forgetting he's even there. I say goodbye and hang up the phone, heaving a deep sigh. Only one day back in Tanner Springs, and I feel like the four-plus years I've been away never happened. I'm back to fighting my way out of the shadow of Triple A Abbott.

A wave of anger wells up in me, followed by a wave of reluctant sympathy. In many ways, my father is a bastard. But he *is* my father. I lie back on the bed for a moment, staring at the cracked ceiling. Dad has changed so much over the years. I remember how it was when I was young. When my mom was still alive. He was so different back then. Oh, he was still a wheeler-dealer, someone who always strove for power and recognition. But still, he was so *proud* back then. Proud of his family, proud of his beautiful wife, proud of his new political career.

Now, despite the hard exterior he presents to the world, there's an undercurrent of loneliness and paranoia that I always notice whenever I talk to him. To the rest of the world, he probably still seems like the same old Abe Abbott. But to me, underneath all the bravado, he just seems… a little *broken*. I'm not quite sure when or why it got so bad — maybe it was a combination of things. But I'm almost positive about when it started: my mother's death.

Chapter 5
JENNA

My mother, Maria Abbott, died six years ago. It was a single-car crash, the cause of which was never quite determined. Mom was in the car alone, on a winding highway heading east, about ten miles outside of Tanner Springs. No one knows why she was out there, or where she was going.

Since the accident happened in the middle of the day with no other traffic around, the police suspected drugs or alcohol as the cause at first. But the medical examiner found no trace of anything in her system. Unfortunately, neither did the mechanics who were called in to check the car for any evidence of a malfunction. The only clue as to what might have happened were a couple of sets of skid marks on the highway in the thousand feet or so before her car plunged off the road and down the cliff. Both sets of marks were determined to come from her tires. The most the police could determine was that something seemed to have alarmed her and caused her to begin driving erratically.

About a week or so after her death, Gabriel happened to overhear my father on the phone in his home office. As Gabe stood outside the closed door, he heard Dad saying to someone that he thought the Iron Spiders were behind my mother's death. That they had run her off the road on purpose, as payback to my dad.

The Iron Spiders are a rival MC to the Lords of Carnage. Their territory butts up against the Lords' territory to the south. Apparently my dad suspected the Spiders had targeted my mom as payback for him striking a deal with the Lords, instead of helping them to get a foothold in Tanner Springs. Of course, nothing could be proved either way. Whatever had happened on that road was a secret Mom took with her to her grave, and the Iron Spiders sure as hell weren't talking. But my father, whether or not he was correct, would have to live with the knowledge that his shady business dealings may have killed my mother for the rest of his life.

Hearing my father's theory about Mom's death changed Gabriel. Not long after, he started hanging around the Lords. He prospected for the club with a dedication and determination I'd never seen him display before — in part or in whole, I knew, out of a desire for revenge against the Iron Spiders.

My brother got patched into the Lords of Carnage about a year later, and became "Angel" instead of Gabriel. But the truth about my mother's killer or killers, if she was in fact murdered, has never come to light.

For the thousandth time in six years, I force myself to stop thinking about my mother's death — to stop wondering how different life might be today if she'd never been killed. What would have become of all of us, if Maria Abbott was still here to be my father's wife, and Gabe's and my mom.

I close my eyes and take a deep breath, letting it out slowly to calm myself. Then I sit up, shake my head to clear it, and go back to my job search.

Half an hour of scanning employment websites later, I see nothing I can reasonably apply to. Tanner Springs isn't a very big town, and a lot of the jobs being advertised are for specialized jobs like a physical therapist, or a nurse's aide, or an electrician. No jobs for a college dropout single mom whose only actual skill is pouring drinks.

I'm starting to feel kind of depressed and hopeless, but just then the music of Noah's childish laughter floats toward me from the living room, cutting into my black thoughts.

I smile to myself at the sound, but then the reality that I have a young child to support starts a cold pit of worry forming in my stomach. I don't know what I'm going to do if I don't find something to pay the bills, and quickly. The rent over this tattoo parlor is cheap, but cheap isn't free.

My mind starts to swirl with ever more dire "what if" scenarios. What if I can't find a job at all? What if I have to swallow my pride and move in with my dad? What if I never manage to get back on my feet, and I end up being the town loser, the pathetic shut-in that everyone clucks about in sympathy whenever I walk by?

Enough, I tell myself sternly, and stand up. The situation might be tough, but I'm not going to accomplish anything more by tying myself in knots. I run a distracted hand through my hair, and glance at myself in the small, cracked mirror above my dresser. Then I call to Noah to get ready to go to the park, determined to give him a few hours of uninterrupted attention — even as I wonder to myself what the hell to do next.

Chapter 6
CAS

Rocco "Rock" Anthony, the President of the Lords of Carnage, slams his gavel on the heavy oak table, announcing that the meeting is coming to order.

"All right, you fuckin' savages," he calls above the din. "Settle the fuck down. It's payday."

A chorus of loud cheers greets his announcement, and then Rock turns the meeting over to Geno, the club treasurer.

Geno stands, his massive, barrel-chested body barely fitting in between the chairs and the wall behind us. Picking up a stack of white envelopes, he starts to hand out our earnings. One by one, he barks our names and slides one of the envelopes into our hands, each with our names written in his recognizable chicken-scratch.

By the time he gets around to me, some of the men are already starting to grumble. "A little fuckin' light again this month, isn't it?" Brick, our enforcer, growls. He's holding his slim envelope in his hand like he's weighing it on a scale.

"No shit," Hawk agrees. "Christ, how the fuck much are we down this month? I was expecting…" — he peers into his envelope — "Shit, at least twice this much."

Geno hands me my pay, which barely weighs anything in my hand, then runs a thick hand over his bald pate. "Yeah, it ain't quite what we expected, brothers. There's a couple reasons…"

"The protection deal for the new commercial development on the west side fell through," Rock says flatly. "The developer got spooked."

"God damn it," Skid explodes, his thick brows frowning in anger. "I got bills to fuckin' pay. My kid needs goddamn braces, the old lady says. How the fuck are we supposed to make ends meet like this?"

A few other voices join him, and a low murmur of dissatisfaction reverberates through the chapel. "Look," Rock frowns, looking around at all of us. "I get it. I got stiffed this month, too. We're all in this together. And know that if any of you are going through some tough financial times right now, the club's got your back. I can dig into the reserves if necessary — though I'm gonna be honest with you, there ain't much in it right now."

"We gotta figure out some other way of making money," Gunner says, cutting through the grumbling. "What we got going right now isn't working. We need something more stable. Recession-proof. What with a bunch of the local businesses closing to the larger retailers, the protection shit isn't as lucrative as it used to be."

"Pussy," Horse growls. "The pussy trade's goddamn as recession-proof as they come." He grins. "And you can't go to a big box store to get it."

"Truth," agrees Skid with a short bark of laughter.

Rock's voice rises above the others. "You seriously want to get balls deep, no pun intended, in running a whorehouse?" he counters. "Christ, the entire town of Tanner Springs would shit themselves. We're trying to keep an amicable relationship with the esteemed citizens of our city here, brothers."

"The *women* of Tanner Springs would shit themselves," Horse corrects him with a leer. "The men would be just goddamn fine with it, I wager. Besides, I ain't talking about a whorehouse. I'm talking about a 'gentlemen's club.'" Raucous laughter and knowing jeers ensue. "What?" he says, feigning shock. "Are you implying that we don't require our customers to wear a suit and tie? I intend to offer only the highest caliber of pussy to our esteemed clientele."

"The women of Tanner Springs should appreciate it, too," Skid sneers. "The hot ones, anyway. We'd be providing employment. They wouldn't have to work retail for barely minimum wage. Dancing is good tips."

"You know that from experience, pretty boy?" Hawk snorts.

Brick pipes up then. "You know what? I'm all for this. Shit, we could use some new blood around here, too. The club whores are gettin' a little stale for my tastes."

"If you guys wanna do this," Horse says, turning to him, "I got an in. Buddy of mine down in Elk River's got a place. Calls it Cherry Pie's. The fucker's making bank, too." He shrugs. "We could open up a Cherry Pie's, Tanner Springs branch."

"Let's do it," Brick urges, looking around the table. "What do you fuckers think?"

"Whoa, whoa, whoa," Rock says, spreading his hands. "It's a little quick to go from 'we need some extra income' to 'let's start a pussy farm' in five minutes, brothers."

"We gotta do something, Rock," Tank challenges. "If this protection deal fell through, then where's the money coming from next month? Or the month after that? Or the month after that?"

"Look. I'm not saying no way. I'm saying that we'd be stupid to rush into something without thinking it through first, just because we need cash," Rock bites out. "We have a stable situation with the people of Tanner Springs right now.

We throw something together like this, it could upset a delicate balance here."

"Yeah," snorts Brick. "It's the *people of Tanner Springs* you're worried about."

Rock cuts him a look of barely concealed anger. "You got something to say, you say it, brother."

"I said what I had to say." Brick's voice rises a notch. For a couple of beats, there's complete silence in the room. To my right, I can hear Gunner's breathing.

"I say we put it to a vote," Angel finally says in a loud voice, cutting through the silence. Rock flicks his eyes away from Brick, but says nothing.

"Second," Horse nods.

Rock's face turns dark. "Okay. We vote. All in favor of going forward with starting up a pussy business, raise your hands."

Hands go up, and a chorus of ayes, with Brick's voice the loudest. I've seen him argue with Rock before, but it's unusual to see our Enforcer clash so openly with the President.

"All those opposed," Rock growls, raising his hand. He looks around the room.

The rest of the hands go up, including Geno's, Gunner's, and mine. It's not that I'm opposed to the idea, but I've never been the type to rush into a room without knowing where the exits are. Angel's been sitting motionless, lost in thought, during the vote. Finally, he slowly raises his hand as well.

"The nays have it, by two votes," Rock barks, a glint in his eye. A low grumble of anger is the only response. "We'll revisit this later, brothers. I hear you that we need to find some alternative sources of income. Anyone with any good ideas that we should look into, come see me."

Church continues, with a couple other items of business that are less charged in nature, but the mood in the room stays tense. Eventually, we've run through everything that needs to be dealt with, and Rock looks around the room. "Any other new business? Hearing none…"

"Move to adjourn," Brick says, his tone flat. He barely waits until Hawk seconds him before he's out the door and heading toward the bar.

"Well, that fuckin' went well," Gunner mutters next to me as we stand to leave.

Chapter 7
CAS

Back out in the bar, the welcome home party I had been anticipating has pretty much soured. Around the room, a lot of pissed off brothers throw back shots and drain their beers, faces tense. I take a step toward Brick and Hawk, ignoring the warning look Brick shoots me.

"Hey, brother, no hard feelings," I say to him, lifting my chin. "I just think we need to think things through a little before we go jumping feet first into a whole other type of business venture."

"That's the fuckin' problem with this club under Rock," Brick mutters. "We sit around and think. Meanwhile, we're letting all sorts of opportunities pass us by, and getting paid shit for it."

Whoa. These words are damn near mutinous, coming from Brick. I've never heard him express such open dissatisfaction with our Prez.

"It isn't like we don't know what's really driving him on this," Hawk agrees, his eyes hard and dark. "God fuckin' forbid that anything happens in this town that hurts Abe fuckin' Abbott's chances of getting reelected."

Oh, so that's what it is. I knew there were a few members of the Lords who are less than thrilled with what they see as Rock's tying the club's fortunes to the mayoral campaign of Abe Abbott. And frankly, I can't completely say I blame them. Abe's been promising the Lords all sorts of perks if he gets reelected for a while now. Rock's been keeping our less legitimate business out of sight and using the club's manpower to make sure things in Tanner Springs run smooth as a top to help the campaign. But so far the club hasn't seen shit in return, as far as I can tell.

As we stand there, Skid comes over, a look of disgust on his face. "What the fuck am I supposed to do with this?" he spits, waving his thin envelope with a sneer. "This shit barely pays my rent for the month."

"Yeah," Hawk nods glumly. "There's gonna be more than one guy looking for ways to supplement his income, if this continues."

Taking on side gigs without club approval is a no-go. But if things continue like they're going, I'm not sure how Rock will be able to say no to it.

Skid shakes his head. "No shit. Next thing you know, I'll be working as a fucking mall cop to make ends meet."

I grin and try to lighten the mood a little. "No offense, brother, but you are *not* getting a job as a mall cop," I say, nodding toward the wall of tattoos running up and down both of his arms and up his neck.

As Skid opens his mouth to reply, a shout erupts from the other side of the room. I look up just in time to see Angel stand up from his bar stool, fists clenching angrily. Facing him is Horse, his shoulders squared like he's looking for a fight.

"Goddamn it, not again," Skid mutters.

"What do you mean?" I ask.

"Shit's been pretty tense since you've been gone," he tells me. "This is the third fight in as many weeks. Brothers are just pissed. Feeling the money squeeze, I guess. Needing to blow off steam."

Ah. Well, that explains the bruises I saw on some of the brothers in church.

"What the fuck do you care, man?" Horse is shouting at Angel. "Of course you fucking voted no. Your *daddy* can always float you the cash, as long as he's still the goddamn mayor."

"Are you *fucking* questioning my loyalty to this club?" Angel shouts. He's so fucking furious that veins are popping out of his neck.

"Oh, shit," I murmur, and set down my beer to stride toward them.

Before I can get there, though, all hell breaks loose. Horse, already half in the bag, throws a wild punch at Angel, catching him in the shoulder. The only reason it connects at all is because there's a table in the way so Angel can't duck. Angel roars with anger and launches himself at Horse, knocking him to the ground with a crash of splintering wood.

Sarge moves in, and tries to pull Angel off Horse. But before he can, Beast, who's the biggest of us all, throws himself into the fray and throws Sarge backwards like he's no heavier than a sack of potatoes. As he does, Jewel, who's carrying a bottle of whiskey and trying to get out of the way, is slammed hard against the counter before anyone can stop her.

The sound of shattering glass and Jewel's piercing cry slice through the brawl like a knife. In a heartbeat, Angel scrambles up and stands, leaving Horse sprawled on the ground. "Fuck, Jewel," he says as he stares at her hand. "Shit."

We all look. Her wrist and the meat of her palm are cut deeply, blood pulsing out of the wound rhythmically. It looks like she might have hit a vein. Jewels stands there for a second, staring dumbly at her hand as though it belongs to someone else. The, just as one of the men yells for a towel, her legs buckle under her. Angel catches her, lowering her gently to the ground, and then Sarge is there, wrapping her wrist tightly to stanch the flow of blood.

"Jesus Christ. Let's get her to a goddamn hospital," Rock's voice comes from behind me. I turn. "Beast. Gunner. Help me load her into the van." His face is a mask of anger. "The rest of you, settle your bullshit while I'm gone."

Beast bends down and lifts Jewel in his arms, then carries her out the door as the rest of us look on. I glance over at Angel, who swears softly and looks down.

"Shit, I feel bad about that," he murmurs. "Jewel's one of the good ones, you know? She pours a mean drink, and she keeps her mouth shut."

"She'll be okay, brother," I half-laugh. "She's not gonna die. The docs at the hospital will patch her up, and she'll be back to work. And you know the club will make sure she's got enough to live on until then."

"Yeah," Angel nods. "I suppose." He looks up at me, and gives me a rueful smile. "Meantime, looks like we'll be pouring our own drinks for a while. We're not gonna find another girl like that so easily."

Chapter 8

JENNA

It's the fifth of the month.

I still don't have a damn job.

I know it's the fifth of the month because the landlord, whose unfortunate name is Charlie Hurt, comes by specially today to inform me of this.

And to remind me that rent was due on the first.

As if I didn't know.

Charlie Hurt is somewhere between forty-five and sixty-five years old. It's almost impossible to tell because he has the kind of fat, flaccid body that comes from years of sitting motionless in front of a television screen with a beer in his hand. It's the end of summer, but his skin is as pale as if we were in Minnesota in February. His sparse, mud-colored hair sticks up from his shiny head in patches. His faded Hawaiian shirt is wrinkled and worn. There's a suspicious stain on his ill-fitting Bermuda shorts.

He's standing at the top of the rickety outdoor stairway that leads to my apartment, on the small landing. I'm blocking the doorway, so he won't come in, because truth be told, he kind of creeps me out. He is not happy about this. As we speak, he keeps casting his eyes inside with a suspicious frown, as though he thinks I'm cooking meth in here or something.

"You know, I only agreed to let you have this month to month lease as a personal favor to your daddy," he's saying to me now. His pasty features twist into a smug, self-satisfied look that tells me he thinks that he and "my daddy" are big buddies now. "Usually, I ask for a six-month lease on this place."

I have to suppress the urge to laugh. I can't imagine anyone being willing to sign a document saying that they are actually *planning* to stay in this rat hole for six months. Instead of laughing, though, I take a deep breath and force myself to be as pleasant as I can. "I appreciate that, Mr. Hurt. Truly I do."

"Call me Charlie," he smirks at me, like he's doing *me* a favor now by letting me call him by his first name. It's all I can do not to roll my eyes.

"Mr. Hurt," I say again, ignoring the flash of anger in his eyes that I'm not calling him *Charlie*. "I promise you, I'll get the rent for you as soon as I possibly can. I have a few job interviews lined up, and…"

"You mean, you don't even have a job yet?" he asks, raising his eyebrows skeptically.

Actually, I'm totally lying about the job interviews, but I'm not about to tell him that. "Mr. Hurt," I try again, "I promise you, I'll have you the rent within the next week. I'm just trying to make sure the money I do have lasts until then. In the meantime, could you maybe apply part of the security deposit toward this month?" I give him what I hope is a convincing smile. "And I can reimburse you for it just as soon as my first paycheck comes in." Either the club or my dad gave him the security deposit before I moved in, but I had insisted on coming up with the rent money myself. Now I'm regretting that, even though I don't want to be more beholden to them than I already am.

The truth is, though, I don't see any hope at all on the horizon of coming up with any more money. I currently have exactly twenty-four dollars and fifty-eight cents in my purse, and another ninety dollars in the bank. And I have no idea when I'll manage to get more. Hell, I even accepted an invitation to come over to my dad's house for dinner tonight because that means one more meal for Noah and me that I won't have to pay for.

Mr. Hurt — *Charlie, ugh* — doesn't seem to even consider my request. I imagine he's had more than one tenant here who's fallen hopelessly behind on the rent.

"Now, why would I do a thing like that?" he says, scoffing. "That security deposit is so's you can't skip out on me and leave me high and dry."

"I know, I know," I say, trying again. "But I promise you, I wouldn't —"

You know," he drawls, interrupting me. "If you can't manage to scrape together the rent, we're just gonna have to figure out some other way for you to pay me. *If* you want to stay here," he adds with a small, creepy grin. His eyes leave my face and travel downward, lingering here and there in a way that makes me want to throw up. It feels almost like he's *touching* me with his gross, feminine hands, bits of dirt visible under the fingernails.

I push down a shudder and get angry instead. "How dare you!" I say, my voice rising in indignation. Then I remember that Noah is right inside, playing a game on my laptop. Drawing myself up to my full height, I continue, my voice low and sharp. "Remember who my father is, *Mister* Hurt. And who my brother is. You suggest *anything* like that again, and you'll come to regret it. Do you hear me?"

A flicker of hatred crosses his face, followed by fear. "That rent is due in five days," he hisses at me, narrowing his eyes. "You don't pay it to me in full by the tenth, you're out. You hear me?"

Before I can think of a response, he is gone, the staircase shaking slightly as he lumbers down it.

When he's finally disappeared into his house, I take a step out on the landing and close my eyes. "Damn," I whisper to myself. "Damn, damn." I *hate* that I just used my family name like that. I hate even more that it was my only choice. I open my eyes again and stare off at a small clump of trees across the street. *I have no power on my own,* I realize. *I have nothing on my own.*

Dejectedly, I sink down on the top step, and try not to cry. My hand goes to my neck, and I begin to finger the ring that's on the chain around my neck for comfort. It's my mother's engagement ring — the only thing I have left of her, except for a couple of faded photographs. My father gave it to me the day after her funeral. I wear it pretty much all the time. It's comforting, almost like she's still here with me, in a way. Unfortunately, right now, it's just making me miss her even more. *Oh, Mom,* I think desperately. *Why is life so hard all the time? Why can't I just get a little break now and then?*

"Mommy?" Noah's voice calls to me. "What did that man want?"

"Nothing, bug," I call back. Tears prick my eyes. *Thank God Noah's still little,* I think. Thank God he's still too young to know how poor we are, and how desperate I am.

With a sigh, I heave myself up and go back into the apartment, into the tiny living room that seems impossibly dim and dingy. Noah is happily playing his game, pumping his tiny fist in joy whenever he gets a point. All the light in this place shines from him. My heart swells with love to the point that it's almost unbearable.

Not trusting my voice for a second, I sit down beside him and hug him to me, burying my face in his brown curls and taking in the still-babyish scent of his skin. *He's growing up so fast,* I think to myself. *I have to make things better for him.* I *have* to make a better life for him. Before he's old enough to see everything we don't have.

As if he senses I'm thinking about him, he looks up at me with his deep brown eyes and flashes me a wide grin that reminds me almost painfully of his father. For a moment, I feel a spike of fear. Anyone who looked at Noah — who *really* looked at him — would see in an instant the resemblance between them. They'd see the hint of a dimple in his left cheek; the wide, intelligent forehead; the deep brown eyes. *What are the odds that I can keep this a secret forever?* I think. *I should never have come back to Tanner Springs.*

As I sit there, holding my boy close, his little tummy starts to growl.

"You hungry, bug?" I ask him, ruffling his hair.

"Yeah," he admits. His eyes light up as he gives me his most winning grin. "Can we go get ice cream?"

It's on the tip of my tongue to say no, but I stop myself. After all, what's one ice cream? I still have twenty-four dollars and fifty-eight cents. It's hardly anything, but it's enough money to bring some joy to a little boy's heart. If I don't get anything but a coffee for myself, treating Noah will cost me less than three bucks.

"You know, what?" I say. "Sure. Let's go get you some ice cream."

Noah lets out an elated yell and bounces up off the couch like he has springs on his feet. It makes me laugh. Which makes me realize I haven't laughed in a while. Determined to let go of my problems for an hour and just be Noah's mom, I grab my purse and lock up the apartment. We descend the staircase to my car, Noah carefully navigating the steep steps, and I push away the thought that I'm needlessly wasting gas. Then I drive us the two miles to the Downtown Diner, which is the only place I can think of that serves ice cream.

I haven't been to the Downtown in years. Since I was in high school, in fact. But as always seems to be the way with diners like this, the Downtown is timeless, and everything is pretty much the same as I remember it. Noah and I slide into a booth, and soon the waitress appears, holding a plastic cup full of crayons for Noah. I order a cup of black coffee for myself and a bowl of chocolate ice cream for him, and Noah gets to work drawing all over the placemat.

As we wait for our order, I scan the mostly-empty diner, and notice that there are voices coming from the back room. Curious, I look over, and what I see makes my blood go hot and cold at the same time.

It's a group of Lords, in their leather cuts.

And in the middle of them is Cas Watkins.

Chapter 9

CAS

It's funny how quickly life returns to normal after you've been gone for a while. It didn't even take me a week to fall back into my normal routine like I'd never been gone at all.

I'm making my usual protection rounds, going around to all the businesses we watch out for and getting updates from the owners. I've pretty much finished the rounds, and ended up here at the Downtown Diner, where a bunch of the brothers are already gathered for a big, greasy hangover breakfast-for-lunch. The partying last night at the clubhouse got a little out of hand, even for us, and more than a few of the men must have some wicked hangovers.

Last night was a good thing for the club, though. After the tensions of the past few weeks, it seemed like last night the fever seemed to break a little, and we were back to partying like brothers. Like a family. I have no illusions that some of the hard feelings about which direction to look for new business have evaporated. I know that's not the case. But I'm hoping they're not a sign of a bigger rift to come.

We're sitting around a big table in the back of the diner, and Tweak is telling some fucking ridiculous story — probably half made-up — about some guy he went to high school with who got pulled over for speeding when he'd been drinking.

"The stupid fucker put a handful of change in his mouth, because someone had told him that copper and silver make the smell of alcohol go away," Tweak is saying, already laughing and shaking his head. "Turns out, he can't get the coins out of his mouth before the cop shows up and has him roll down his window. So when the cop starts asking him questions, the guy starts choking and spitting the coins out of his mouth like a slot machine!"

Tweak barely gets the last words out before he's shaking with laughter, slamming his hand down on the table like he can't get his breath. The other guys are laughing, too, because watching Tweak tell his stories is almost always more entertaining than the stories themselves.

Anyway, it's still good to be there laughing with the brothers, even if I'm mostly laughing because Tweak's full of shit. He's swearing up and down, insisting it's true, when I happen to glance over and see a girl sitting at a booth over by the front door.

For a second my brain doesn't quite register who it is. Then I realize why.

It's Jenna Abbott. There's no mistaking that body.

But her hair's s totally different. It's a dark brown, instead of the honey blond I remember her having. She must have dyed it.

It looks... *good*. Hot, even. My dick thickens in my pants in agreement with my brain.

But it's weird to see her as a brunette. So even though I *know* it's her, I keep staring, then trying not to stare and looking away, then cutting my eyes back at her and staring again.

The years have definitely been good to her. She's changed a little bit — the angles in her face are a little more pronounced, and she's lost some of her adolescent softness. Her waist is slimmer, her breasts fuller. But one thing is the same: she's still a fucking knockout.

Something else has changed, too — so subtle that at first I don't notice it. It's something about the way she's holding herself. Tightly, almost like she's afraid she'll shatter. She sits, almost ramrod straight, the cup of coffee she's ordered clutched in both hands. The way she's holding that mug, it looks like she's almost afraid it will fly away if she lets go of it.

This isn't the carefree girl I remember from when we were kids, I can tell right away. The girl who never seemed to take anything all that seriously. This Jenna looks like she's carrying the weight of the whole world on her shoulders. Looking at her now, it makes me wonder what life has done to her in the last five years, to change her like this. It makes me wish I could turn back time for her, and make all the bad things go away.

At first, I think Jenna hasn't noticed me or the brothers back here. I feel myself gathering my legs under me, getting ready to go up and say hello to her. Then, just as I'm shifting my weight, she glances over. Somehow, just by the way she locks eyes with me, I realize she knew I was here all along. I give her a slight nod and she nervously looks away toward the other side of the booth. I start to stand, and my eyes follow hers to see what she's looking at.

And realize that I've been staring at her so intently I didn't even see there's someone else sitting there with her.

It's a little boy, with brown hair. He's coloring on a placemat. A small bowl with a spoon in it is sitting next to him.

Her kid. Just like Angel said. Somehow, seeing her like that, I'd forgotten.

And then, for some reason, I shift my weight back into my chair and don't go over.

Chapter 10

CAS

The murmur of my brothers' voices washes over me as I continue to sit there in silence. In my mind's eye, I flash back to the last time I saw Jenna. It's almost five years ago now. Hard to believe.

Jenna came back to Tanner Springs for the summer at the end of her freshman year at the university. Somehow, even though Jenna has always been smart as hell, she'd managed to flunk out of college. She came back to town with her tail between her legs, swallowing her pride to face up to her father's wrath.

It was funny: Jenna had never been much of a wild thing when she was younger, but that summer she seemed completely changed. She spent a hell of a lot of nights partying with whichever group of friends she happened to be out with, and because of that, our paths crossed more than a few times.

Looking back on it now, it was probably inevitable that we were going to hook up eventually. Jenna and I had been circling around each other for years, truth be told. By then, I'd been around the block with enough girls that I could usually tell by just a glance when one of them was waiting for me to make a move. With Jenna, it was a little tougher, but I'd catch a little flicker of something in her eye, or see the way her lips parted when she knew I was looking at her. She had the most fuckable goddamn mouth I had ever seen. When she was around, all I could think about was what it would feel like to have those full, pouty lips wrapped around my cock. And judging from the way she looked at me, I was pretty sure she was willing.

I wasn't wrong.

I ran into her one night at a big-ass bonfire someone had set up at an abandoned farmhouse outside of town. It was the end of August — way too hot for a bonfire — and the night had one of those end-of-summer blowout feels to it. I knew from Gabe that Jenna had pulled her shit and her money together over the summer and managed to get herself enrolled at a community college about an hour away, to try to make up the credits she'd lost by failing out at the state university. That night, she acted like she was looking for a last hurrah, as well.

Normally, Jenna didn't drink all that much when she partied — though she would dance with a wild abandon you couldn't help but admire — but she seemed like she was a couple beers in when she strode up to me in the dark with a saucy smirk on her face and a challenge in her eye.

"Haven't seen you around much these past few weeks, Cas Watkins." Her chin lifted toward me, her mouth slightly open in that tempting pout that always made me want to pull her lips down onto my waiting cock.

It was true, I hadn't been around much. I'd stopped going to as many parties with the townies I'd gone to high school with. I'd recently begun prospecting with the Lords of Carnage, and the club was taking up a lot of my time.

"I didn't figure you'd notice," I drawled back at her, curving my lips into a lazy grin that I knew from experience drove girls wild.

Jenna blushed, but the alcohol made her bold. "I'm leaving town tomorrow." Glancing over toward where all our vehicles were parked, she added, "How about taking me for a ride on that motorcycle of yours?"

It was my first bike, an old but serviceable Harley that I'd gotten for free from one of my uncles who wanted to get it out of his garage.

"You sure you're in shape to take a ride?" I teased her, nodding toward the beer.

"This is only my second one," she protested, holding it up to show me. "And besides. I won't be the one driving." Jenna took a step toward me, until she was close enough that

I could smell the faint perfume of her shampoo. "I trust you," she said softly.

I was used to girls throwing themselves at me — even flat-out propositioning me — but with Jenna it kind of threw me for a loop. I'd spent so much mental energy keeping a wall up between me and her because of her brother that having it knocked down like that knocked me off my guard a bit. My cock jumped in my pants as I imagined how it would feel to have her body tight against my back as we rode.

"You ever been on a bike before?" I asked her.

"No," she breathed, looking into my eyes. Suddenly, it somehow felt like we were talking about something else. "But you know what to do. You'll teach me."

I put her on the back of my bike and took her out into the country, driving just fast enough that she clung to me and pressed her breasts against my back as we rode. My cock was like a fucking iron rod the whole time, and by the time we arrived at the lot with the old motor home a distant cousin of mine used as a hunting cabin sometimes, any final resolve I was hanging onto had melted away into the night.

I broke the lock on the motor home, pulled Jenna inside, and took her once, then twice, the two of us writhing and clutching at each other until we were both drenched with sweat and exhausted. Eventually, we fell asleep, with her in my arms, and didn't wake up again until right before dawn. I took her once more before we left, then drove her back to town. I dropped her off a block away from her house, and she kissed me deep and long before dashing off through a neighbor's yard toward her back door.

The next day, she caught holy hell from her dad about staying out all night. I heard about it from Angel, who of course had no idea that it was me she'd been out with, or what she'd been doing. To this day, I've never told him. And I don't plan to. It was maybe the best night and the best sex I've ever had in my life — the culmination of years of pent-up feelings and desires. But both Jenna and I knew it was a bad idea. A mistake. Even though it felt better than any other mistake I've ever made, before or since.

Sarge's bark of laughter as one of the brothers tells a joke brings me out of my reverie. With a start, I glance over at Jenna's booth to see that she's paid her bill and is standing up. She holds out her hand, and the little boy takes it. Together, the two of them walk out the door. My throat constricts a little as I watch them leave. I'm not sure why.

I should have said hello, I think. Well, fuck it. I'll wait for the right time, whenever that might be.

* * *

Back at the clubhouse, I can't stop thinking about Jenna. I'm hanging out at one of the low top tables with Angel, playing Texas Hold'em and drinking beer. Jewel's still out with her fucked up hand, so one of the prospects is behind the bar, looking kind of harried.

"The board gives me a straight flush," I announce, laying my cards out on the table.

"God*damn*," Angel swears, throwing his hand down in disgust. "That's the third hand in a row you've won."

"You sure you don't wanna play with one of the prospects?" I kid him. "Up your chances?"

"Fuck off," Angel tosses back. He moves to grab up the deck when Rock's voice explodes toward us from over near the bar.

"Are you fuckin' *kidding* me?" Rock yells. "How hard can it be to make a Red Rooster? It's just fucking beer and tomato juice!" He flings the glass he's drinking from toward the floor, emptying its contents with a splash, then slams the mug back down on the bar so loud the prospect jumps a mile high.

Angel snorts. "I don't know how he can drink that shit," he mutters.

"Just give me a goddamn beer!" Rock bites out. The shaking prospects reaches for the empty glass, and Rock explodes again. "Give me a *fucking clean glass!*"

"Holy hell," I chuckle. "That prospect must be pissing himself." I'm guessing some of this is just for show, to test the prospect's mettle. But Rock is definitely particular about his drinks.

And then, as Angel and I are chuckling at the show in front of us, the germ of an idea takes hold in my brain.

"Hey," I say, leaning over. "Didn't you say your sister was a bartender in the city?"

"Yeah," Angel replies absently, and then his face transforms into a frown. "Wait. Are you seriously suggesting my sister should be a club girl?" His fist tightens around his beer bottle.

"Fuck, brother, not a *club girl*," I laugh, spreading my hands. "A *bartender*. Hey, you said she needs a job. And she's your sister. Nobody here will touch her."

Chapter 11

JENNA

Three days and endless applications later, I still have no job and I'm feeling more desperate than I ever have in my life.

It's time to do something I hoped I'd never have to do.

Sam's Pawn Shop is about half a mile away from downtown in an aging strip mall, between a nail place and a sad little coffee shop that never has any customers. It's the only place in town I can think of to do this. I hate the thought of coming here, because I know Sam from when I was a kid. Back then, he used to own an appliance repair place, and my dad swore he'd never buy his appliances from anywhere else. Of course, when the big box stores started moving into Tanner Springs, little places like Sam's shop couldn't compete, and he had to close down. So now, he does this instead.

I take Noah with me to the pawn shop. Partly it's because I don't have anyone to leave him with. But partly it's because I'm hoping Noah will distract Sam from asking too many prying questions.

I pull into the parking lot of the strip mall, and easily find a spot right in front of Sam's shop. After helping Noah out of his car seat, I square my shoulders and put on a bright, carefree smile. Then I push open the door and say a quick prayer.

Sam is sitting at the counter clipping his fingernails when I walk in. He looks up, startled, like he's not all that used to having people walk into the shop. It's clear he doesn't recognize me, though he's eyeing me like he's trying to figure out if he knows me. Granted, he hasn't seen me in many years. Plus, my hair is a different color now. My heart jumps a little: maybe I can get through this whole thing without him realizing who I am. Then I realize that I probably have to give him my name and my ID if I want to be able to get my pawned item back, and my heart sinks a little again.

"Hi," I say. I decide not to give him any hints yet. "I have something I'd like to pawn." *Duh. Of course I do. What a dumb way to start.* I smile, too wide, to compensate for sounding like an idiot. "It's this ring."

Reaching into my pocket, I take out the small box where I've put my mother's engagement ring. It almost broke my heart to take it off the chain around my neck. I was afraid I'd start crying in the pawn shop if I did it here, so I left the chain at home and brought the ring like this instead.

Sam is still peering at me curiously, his head cocked, when he takes the ring from me. He breaks my gaze and looks at it, holding it up to the light. "Nice," he remarks. "Wedding ring?"

"Engagement," I correct him. "Not mine." He looks at me sharply. "I mean, it was my mother's," I stammer. "The ring belongs to me, though."

A flicker of something crosses his features. Recognition? If it is, he doesn't say anything. For a moment, he says nothing. Then: "Hold on just a second. I'll be right back."

He leaves the ring on the counter in front of me and disappears into the back of the store. I wait for two minutes, three minutes, trying to be patient. Noah gets tired of waiting by my side and wanders off to stare at the rows of chain saws, guitars, amplifiers, and electronics.

Sam comes back out. "Stay put," he tells me. "I'm having an appraiser come to look at the ring."

I frown at him. That seems odd. The ring is a fairly nice one, but not so nice that I'd think he'd need to have someone else take a look at it. Then again, what do I know? I've actually never pawned anything before. And maybe this means the ring is worth more than I thought.

I put the ring back into the box for safekeeping, and slide it back into my pocket. Wandering over to Noah, I tell him in a low voice to stop putting his hands on the glass case in front of him. I try to figure out some sort of small talk that I can make with Sam, but when I glance back in his direction, I see he's gone back to clipping his nails.

Five more minutes pass. I'm getting kind of antsy, and Noah's asking when we're going to leave. I start to ask Sam how long it will be before the appraiser gets here, but as I do, the low sound of a motorcycle approaching stops me.

Before I know what's happening, I see that Angel is outside the shop, parking his bike in the spot next to my car. Open-mouthed, I look over at Sam accusingly, but he refuses to meet my gaze.

My heart sinks as Angel storms into the shop. "What the fuck, Jenna?" he explodes at me. "What the hell are you doing?"

Well, I guess now I know Sam recognizes me, I think bitterly. Shooting him an angry look, I hiss at Angel, "Can we please not do this here?"

"Fine. Come on." He takes me by the arm and starts to lead me out, but I shake him off. Picking Noah up into my arms, I nod stonily toward the front entrance and follow

Angel out of the pawn shop, shooting daggers at Sam's bald head as I do.

"Why didn't you tell me you needed money this bad?" Angel barks at me when we're out on the sidewalk. "Sam said you were trying to pawn Mom's engagement ring?"

I don't know if he's mad about the ring, or just mad that his sister went to a pawn shop instead of to the family, or both. "Angel, I..." I begin, but I don't know what to say. I don't want Noah to hear any of this. Not that he'd understand, exactly. I know he's too young. But I don't want him to hear that we need money. I don't want my little boy to worry.

"Look, can you just let me put Noah in the car first?" I ask. I open the back door and set him down, and Noah climbs obediently into his car seat. I grab two of his toys, a plastic dune buggy and his stuffed monkey, and hand them to him. Leaving the door open so he won't get too hot, I come back to Angel on the sidewalk.

"Why didn't you tell us?" Angel repeats as soon as I'm back. "Shit, Dad would have given you money. All you would have needed to do was ask. I still don't get why you didn't just move in with him."

"You know what he's like, Angel. I can't." I shake my head in frustration. "I just can't give him the satisfaction of knowing that once again, his daughter is a failure who can't stand on her own two feet." All the frustration and worry of the past few days wells up inside me, and for a second I think

I'm going to cry. "It's bad enough I had to come back here at all. Bad enough that I had to have him put a down the security deposit on the apartment. I just want to make it on my own," I say, closing my eyes against the swell of emotions. "I just want to pay my own way."

I open my eyes again, and heave a deep sigh.

"I don't even know why I'm here, Angel," I say helplessly. "I don't know how things got so… hard."

For a few moments, Angel doesn't say anything. We're not exactly close, and it's not my habit to confide in him about my problems. He seems to be struggling for the right words to say. Finally, he breaks the silence.

"Jenna," he begins slowly, "If you need money this bad, then come pour drinks at the club bar. We've got an opening, and the prospect that's been doing it is shit." He cracks a small grin then. "You'd be doing us a favor, frankly. And the pay's not bad."

My eyes widen. "Are you seriously suggesting that I take a job slinging drinks for an outlaw motorcycle club right now?"

He shrugs. "You need a job. We need a bartender. Why not?"

"No," I blurt out. "No, no, no. I don't want anything to do with the Lords of Carnage, Angel." My temper's rising, but I know part of the reason is that deep down inside of me, there's a tiny little voice inside me saying *It's a lifeline, Jenna. Take it.* I take a deep breath and push the voice away. *No.*

Angel rolls his eyes and tries again. "Jenna. Look. Just please come by. At least check it out before you blow me off." I open my mouth and he cuts me off. "C'mon, don't be like that. Come to the club. Just see it for yourself. Whatever you're thinking, it's not that bad."

I snort.

Angel smirks. "You know, some of the brothers have old ladies and children. We even do charity stuff."

"Yeah, right," I sigh. "I'm sure it's a regular Rotary Club over there."

His laughter is easy. "You'll never know unless you come check it out for yourself. Come on, let's go."

"What, now?" My eyes grow wide. "Are you forgetting that I've got Noah with me?"

"He'll be fine. Trust me. You think I'd bring my sister and my nephew there if you wouldn't be safe?" Angel glances toward my son, who's making his stuffed monkey, Chip-Chip, do back flips. "You can nail my balls to the wall later if anything bad happens," he promises.

Against my better judgment, and muttering to myself about what an idiot I am the whole time, I end up agreeing to follow Angel back to the club. The whole way there, Noah is chattering to himself in the back seat and making monkey sounds, and I wonder to myself if I'm making a huge mistake.

Chapter 12

JENNA

The clubhouse is a nondescript building set back from the main road, with a large, fenced in area to the side and a parking lot in front. Rows of bikes line the portion of the lot next to the fence.

Angel parks his Harley at the end of one of the rows, and walks over to me just as I'm unbuckling Noah from his car seat. I hand my son to his uncle, who awkwardly gets him into a piggyback position, and together we enter the club through a heavy, windowless front door.

What the hell am I doing? I ask myself as Angel swings the door open. I open my mouth to tell him I've changed my mind. But by the time I get my voice to work, he's already through the door and inside the clubhouse with Noah.

It takes a couple of seconds for my eyes to adjust to the light difference, but when I do I see we've entered a large, open room. There are about a dozen large, tattooed men of various shapes and ages, all wearing leather cuts emblazoned with the Lords of Carnage rockers. The men are scattered around the room, standing or sitting, laughing or playing pool. A few women are there, too, which surprises me even though Angel told me there might be. Most of them are dressed in clothes so tight I wonder how they can even breathe, and some of them are wearing makeup more dramatic than I would ever wear even to go out to a club. If I went to clubs, that is.

"Hey, y'all, this is my sister, Jenna," Angel yells. "And her kid, Noah. You treat them with respect."

It occurs to me to wonder what kind of welcome I'd be getting if I *wasn't* the VP's sister. But before I can go too far down that rabbit hole, an enormous — like *unbelievably* enormous — man with a large beard comes up and claps Angel on the shoulder.

"So this is your family, brother," he rumbles, in a voice just as deep as I would have expected. Then he raises his huge, tattooed arm and extends his hand toward Noah.

"Hey there, little man," he says. "I'm Tank."

Noah's eyes are so big I can't tell if he's terrified or just fascinated. "Hi," he says in a small voice, putting his tiny paw in Tank's larger one. They shake solemnly, and damned if it isn't somehow about the cutest thing I've ever seen.

It's surreal. I think this place is already starting to mess with my head.

"Ma'am," Tank then says respectfully, turning to me and nodding his head once.

"Uh, pleased to meet you… Tank," I stammer.

I have to resist a sudden urge to burst into hysterical laughter. I'm exchanging polite pleasantries with a tattooed, leather-clad human mountain who could break me in half with two fingers.

Yup. *Seriously* starting to mess with my head.

Then, from over to one side, one of the women squeals and comes over to us, tottering in thigh-length boots.

"Oh, my gosh, he is just the cutest little thing!" she croons. "I just love kids, and he is just adorable. A real future lady-killer." She winks at Noah and then turns to me. "Hi, I'm Jewel," she says. She starts to lift up a hand for me to shake, but then lowers it quickly. I look down and see it's covered in a thick bandage. "Sorry, I keep forgetting about this thing," she pouts ruefully.

Angel speaks up. "Jewel's the bartender I told you about. She's out of commission for at least a few weeks."

She's pretty, with wheat-colored hair and a wide, toothy smile. Her revealing clothes notwithstanding, there's kind of an innocence about her attitude and demeanor that feels a little strange in an MC clubhouse — well, like I know what an

MC clubhouse should even feel like. But she's not exactly the "rode hard and put away wet" woman I would have imagined.

"What's your name, kiddo?" she's asking Noah now. Normally, it overwhelms him when lots of adults start paying attention to him, and I expect him to shrink back from her. Instead, he gives her a shy smile.

"Noah," he tells her.

"That's such a good name for a handsome boy like you," she grins at him. "How old are you?"

"I'm four," he tells her proudly, holding up his hand to show her how many. "Almost five. I can read already!"

"Wow. That's great. You must be really smart, then."

Noah nods. "I am." We all laugh.

"Your little boy reminds me of my little brother, back in Indiana." Jewel says, looking at me. "He's ten. Going on about thirty."

I chuckle. "Yeah, Noah gives me a run for my money."

"Hey, Jewel," Angel says. "You wanna take Noah for a few minutes? We've got some business to discuss."

"Sure thing!" she says enthusiastically. "Come on, Noah. You want me to teach you a card trick?"

Noah bobs his head up and down, and slides off Angel's back. Jewel immediately offers him her non-bandaged hand and leads him over to one of the couches to play with him.

Angel leads me over to the bar. "And that fucker there, pardon my French, is the reason we need to get you behind the bar," he says, pointing. A handsome but nervous-looking young guy behind the bar gives me a slight wave.

Prospect," he calls to him. "You think you can pour my sister a decent drink without killing her?"

I almost say no to the drink, but the fact is, my nerves are kind of jangled at the moment. I ask for a beer, which is cold and soothing and ends up settling me down a bit. A few more of the MC members come over to see what's going on, and I start to realize I know quite a few of them. Angel makes more introductions, and I let myself relax a little bit. The men aren't nearly as intimidating as I expected them to be, although I'm guessing that's because Angel's my brother. They are, almost to a man, freaking *massive*, though. The smallest of them has almost a foot on me. I don't think I've ever been in a room with such a sea of testosterone before.

It's… freaky, I admit. I mean, most of these guys are objectively *hot*. But thankfully, they seem to be dialing it back with me, and I'm thankful for that. Far from feeling in danger, I actually start to have fun bantering with the men.

About half an hour later, I take a deep breath and turn to Angel.

"I can't believe I'm going to do this," I tell him, "but I accept your offer. Just until I can get on my feet, and Jewel can start tending again," I add hastily.

Angel grins at me. "Good deal. Now, get behind the bar and mix me your fanciest drink."

I snort. "Will do. Where do you keep the paper umbrellas?"

I slip behind the bar and root around to see what they have. I end up mixing him an Irish Car Bomb, which I adorn with a makeshift umbrella that I've made out of a toothpick and a paper coaster. I bring it my brother in the back, where he's started a game of pool with a few of the other men, who laugh and give him shit about the umbrella.

From the corner of my eye, I catch a glimpse of Jewel and Noah. They're playing some sort of card game where they're both slapping the cards on the table as hard as they can. He's laughing and screaming in glee — the happiest I've seen him since we moved to Tanner Springs. I push down my feelings of guilt and allow myself a rare moment of optimism.

Maybe things are going to be okay, I think for the first time in days.

And then, just as I'm walking back to the bar, the front door opens and Cas Watkins strolls in.

Chapter 13

CAS

Even though it was originally my idea for Angel to ask Jenna to tend bar for the MC, it's still a pretty big shock to see her here.

Since that day at the Downtown Diner, I haven't seen Jenna at all. And definitely not this close up.

I could have used a warning.

Again, I'm struck by how startling it is to see her as a brunette. It definitely suits her. Hell, pretty much anything would look good on Jenna, though. She could probably shave her damn head and still be a damn knockout. Even so, it still feels a little… off. Like the way she was carrying herself the other day at the diner. The curtain of hair, and the way she has a tendency to hide behind it, feels like a barrier.

Something she's consciously placing between her and the world.

She looks up at me just as I come through the door and freezes in her tracks. Those pale, pale blue eyes lock onto me, her lips parting slightly in surprise. I take advantage of the moment to check out the entire package close up.

Jenna is petite in stature, barely coming up to my shoulder. But even so, somehow she has legs that just won't quit. She's wearing a pair of jean shorts that are probably meant to be modest, but on her they're anything but. Looking at her now, my eyes raking over her curves, I can still remember how it felt to reach down and cup her ass, pulling her toward me for the first time all those years ago. The *feel* of it in my hands is so strong right now that I have to fight the rising of my cock against my zipper. Shit. No good pitching a tent right here in front of the whole club. Especially when I can't do anything about it.

"Hey," I say, my voice huskier than I mean it to be.

"Hey," she half-whispers back.

"So. You're working here now?"

Jenna blinks her eyes in surprise. "Yeah, I guess so. How did you know?"

"I, uh…" I shrug. "I suggested it to Angel. After Jewel got hurt."

"Oh." Jenna looks flustered, like she doesn't quite know what to make of that. "You did?"

Frankly, neither do I. Oh, yeah, of course I suggested it to Angel. At the time, it just seemed like a practical solution to a mutual problem. But that was when Jenna still seemed kind of… *abstract.* Now, with her here in the flesh, right in front of me… Well, let's just say, I've never been much of a one to resist temptation. And this, right here? This is a *fucking* temptation. And I brought it on myself.

"Yeah," I continue nonchalantly. "It just seemed like it made sense. Angel said you were back in town, and that you were having some money troubles, so…"

Jenna's expression changes, in the space of an instant. Her jaw sets, and her eyes flash. She's embarrassed, and more than that, she's pissed.

"Great. Glad to know my life is and my problems are something everyone feels entitled to know about," she says sharply, giving a short, sarcastic laugh. "But I guess it was probably obvious anyway. Why else would I accept a job in a place like this?"

Fuck. I feel bad. Jenna's always been proud. She doesn't like people to see her weaknesses. I know that much about her. I wish I could take my words back, but of course it's too late for that.

Instead, I pretend to be angry myself, to take the focus off her. "What do you mean, a place like this?" I retort. "You think you're too good for the likes of us?"

It seems to work, at least a little. "No, that's not what I meant," she says quickly.

"Sure it is," I continue. "You think we're just a bunch of criminals. The lowest of the low."

"No!" She rolls her eyes in frustration. "It's just that…" She pauses.

"It's just that what?" I prompt, crossing my arms.

"I just…" She's flustered now, and her blush heats her skin. I resist the urge to reach up and slide my thumb along her jawline, to see if it will make her blush more.

"I'm sorry, you're right," she finally admits. "That was rude of me to say. I don't think badly of the club. I just…" She sighs, looking defeated. "Well, I guess I was hoping to find a job other than bartending for once. I guess I'm just frustrated that I have to basically take a charity job with my brother's club."

"It's not charity," I say gently. "We really do need a bartender. Just so happens, you fit the bill and you're free." Her face looks dubious, and I decide not to push it. I try to change the subject. "How've you been?" I ask her without thinking, and then realize I've just put the focus right back on her and her troubles. *Smooth.*

She laughs softly. "Okay. I mean, apart from the obvious."

"You look good," I say, because it's true. Her blush just gets deeper. Fuck, she's just as goddamn gorgeous and sexy as I remember her being. More, actually. What I wouldn't give to back her against the bar and have my way with her right now.

"Thanks," she murmurs, looking down. "So do you."

Aha.

"Hey, Ghost!" yells Beast from the back. "Get back here and settle a bet for Tank and me."

"Calm your tits," I call back. I grin at Jenna. "Sorry. Pardon my French."

"I forget they call you Ghost now," Jenna says, a tiny smile quirking the corners of her mouth. "Angel told me that." She wrinkles her nose. "It took me a minute to figure out it's because your name is Casper."

"That's not why they call me Ghost," I tell her.

"It's not?"

I take a half-step toward her and lower my voice a notch. "No," I say, "But I can be a very *friendly* ghost, if you want me to."

I mostly say it just to see her reaction, but as soon as the words are out of my mouth, something changes. It's as though an electric arc just shot between us. Her eyes lock onto mine for a long, scorching second. When she finally looks away, I realize I'm hard as a rock.

"I'm just here to pour drinks, Cas," she says quietly.

"Ghost!" Beast shouts again.

"Goddamn it," I mutter, turning away. Jenna retreats behind the bar, and I go back to kick Beast's ass.

Chapter 14

CAS

I try to stay away from Jenna for the rest of her shift, but I'm still hyper-aware of her presence in the clubhouse.

I can't help but keep watching her out of the corner of my eye as she moves around the bar and brings drinks to the brothers. I catch every movement she makes. I notice the way her white T-shirt clings to the curve of her breasts, and a memory of her pert, pink nipples makes me practically bust the zipper on my jeans. I see her leaning over to serve a beer — perfect ass molded by her shorts — and almost come in my pants thinking about how good it would feel to plunge myself deep inside her. It's fucking torture having her here. What's even worse is that every once in a while, I catch her glancing over at me, furtively, like she can't help herself.

It feels just like that summer five years ago. Here we are, dancing around each other again. It's just a matter of time before we stop dancing. I can feel it.

The first hour or so, Jenna's moving around pretty stiffly, like she's not sure what to expect out of the brothers. But eventually, she starts to loosen up as they come to the bar to chat her up and make her laugh. Angel's in back with Rock talking business because we have church later, and it looks like his absence is starting to make some of the brothers feel a little bolder about flirting with her.

A little too goddamn bold, for my taste.

Sarge seems especially taken with our new bartender. I watch from the other side of the bar as he pulls up a stool and starts saying shit to Jenna I can't hear. I see her throw back her head and laugh a few times, and before I know it my blood starts to heat up in my veins. Sarge can be a charming motherfucker when he wants to be, but from what I've heard, his sexual tastes run a little on the violent side. As I watch Jenna roll her eyes and laugh again at something he's just said to her, I know he's making a play for her.

Jenna isn't my old lady. I have no business getting between her and anyone. And hell, I know she's somewhat protected by being Angel's sister. As I watch Sarge flirt with her, I keep repeating these things to myself like a mantra. But even so, my blood starts to simmer, and then to boil.

The idea of Sarge, or any one of these men, bedding her is more than I can handle. By the time she walks by him and he slaps her on the ass, I'm seeing red and too far gone to care. I stand up, knocking my chair to the floor, and before I know it I've crossed the room in three strides.

"Don't you *fucking* touch her!" I snarl. I pull back and punch Sarge hard in the face before he even knows what's happening. He falls backwards off the stool and hits the ground. Getting to his feet with a roar, he lunges for me. Sarge is a little bigger than I am, but I've got adrenaline on my side, and I'm not backing down. He barrels toward me, aiming to plow me down by the waist, but I'm ready for him. I crouch down low and catch him in the chest with an uppercut just as he rams into me. Then we're both on the floor, trying to land punches where we can.

"—it! Stop it! Cas, stop!" Jenna's voice seeps into the fog of rage in my head. I feel myself being pulled off of Sarge by a couple pairs of arms, and I look up to see that Tank and Skid are hauling Sarge up, too.

"What the hell is wrong with you?" Jenna cries, getting in my face like she has no idea how close I am to exploding.

I shake off the brothers holding me and grab Jenna by the arm, pulling her outside without a word as she continues to bitch at me. I'm practically shaking, I'm so angry, and I'm working hard not to take it out on her.

"What are you *doing*, Cas?" Jenna stumbles behind me until I round the far corner of the building, invisible from the parking lot. I turn and face her.

"Sarge should know better than to touch the sister of the VP," I rasp, my jaw clenched tight.

Jenna huffs at me and rolls her eyes. "Oh, for God's sake, Cas. He wasn't going to try anything. He was just being stupid."

"Damn straight, he was being stupid," I mutter. "He's about to get his head bashed in."

"Why do you even care?" she challenges me. "What, are you suddenly the protector of all women? Do you think I can't take care of myself?"

"Of course you can take care of yourself," I scoff. "In most circumstances. But shit, Jenna, this isn't some frat boy we're talking about here."

"Cas." Jenna's clearly starting to lose patience. "Do you think Sarge is the first man to slap me on the ass? I'm a damn bartender. This shit happens to me all the time. I don't like it, but I don't have the luxury of taking it seriously. I need the tip money."

"The next time it happens — no matter who does it — they'll have me to answer to," I growl.

Jenna's eyes widen in surprise. "I don't believe it," she cries, shaking her head. "You're jealous!"

I don't reply, because she's goddamn right I'm jealous.

"No," she says then. "No. You do *not* get to do this."

"Do what?" I mutter.

"Just because we had sex once years ago, you do not get to feel like you have some sort of claim on me, Cas Watkins," she declares, jutting out her chin.

"If memory serves, we fucked more than once," I correct her. My dick jumps at the thought.

That takes her aback for a second, but she squares her shoulders and continues. "You don't own me, Cas."

"Oh no?" I rasp, pulling her to me.

For a second, she resists. But when my mouth comes down on hers, the sound that comes from her isn't a protest, but a moan. We crash back into the wall, and I lift her up, cupping her ass and pressing her thighs apart until the crotch of her jeans is pressed against the aching hardness of my cock. Jenna gasps, and I feel her instinctively buck her hips against me. It's just as fucking good as I remember.

She moans again, more loudly, and slides herself against me, angling her hips so I know she's aching for it, too. Her eyes had closed when I kissed her, but now they open again and stare at me. Her pupils are huge and dark. The look we exchange is electric.

If it wasn't for the fabric between us, I'd be inside her right now.

I practically come at the thought.

I'm considering whether to pull her into the trees and give us what we both want, when a voice calls from around the corner. "Ghost! Church!"

"Fuck," I groan, my lips sliding from Jenna's. "It's Angel." I ease her to the ground and adjust my raging hard-on.

Jenna's flushed and disheveled, her eyes hooded. Her mouth is open slightly, her breath coming in pants. "Shit. You go," she tells me, and takes off in the other direction, toward the back of the clubhouse.

I round the corner to find Angel standing out by the bikes, looking around. "Where you been?" he frowns when he sees me.

"Just went out for a smoke," I lie.

"Where's Jenna?" Angel asks. "Beast said you two walked out together."

"She's, uh…" I see Jenna rounding the corner on the other side of the building. "She's over there. She got mad at me and stormed away."

"Huh." Angel's face is suspicious, but he lets it go. "Okay, well, come on. Rock's ready to get started."

I nod and follow him into the bar, casting a quick glance over at Jenna just before I go inside. Our eyes meet for a second, and then she looks away.

Maybe I don't own her, like she said. But it looks like maybe I still do have a claim on her, after all.

Chapter 15

JENNA

I'm pretty sure what just happened was a bad idea.

Great. Add it to the list.

It didn't *feel* like one, though. God help me, but kissing Cas Watkins just now felt… well, it felt amazing. More than amazing. It felt like coming home.

I take a few more minutes outside after Cas and Angel go back in, to try to get my head on straight. But every nerve ending in my body feels like it's *buzzing* with the memory of his body and the electricity of Cas's touch. The ache between my legs has graduated to a throb, and I almost moan out loud in frustration and need. God only knows what would have happened between us if Angel hadn't come out just now.

No, that's a lie. I know *exactly* what would have happened.

And I wanted it to happen. Hell, I *still* want it to happen. I feel like I'm sliding down the side of a steep hill, careening toward the inevitable. The problem is, I don't know if I should put out my hands and try to stop myself, or just let it happen. Because either way, I'm pretty sure the end result is gonna be the same.

I pace back and forth in the parking lot for a few minutes, which doesn't seem to calm me much but at least gives me something to do. Finally, I blow out a deep breath of frustration, then head back into the clubhouse, before someone comes out here looking for me.

When I get inside, I see that the tables and chairs that were overturned when Cas punched Sarge have been put to rights. Off in one corner, Noah has fallen asleep in Jewel's lap. She's quietly reading a worn-looking paperback, silently turning the pages as his little chest rises and falls.

"Are you okay?" I mouth at her, feeling a twinge of guilt, but she just smiles and nods.

Then, when I walk back to the bar, I find that my tip jar has been stuffed full of bills.

I almost cry with relief and happiness at the unexpected sight. I look around in astonishment, to see who did this, but then I remember all the club members are in a meeting now. "Church," Angel called it for some reason. So, I make a promise to find out who's responsible and thank them for it later.

I empty the jar on the counter and start to count out the bills. *Wow.* There's enough here that with luck and a couple more shifts, I'll be able to make rent before Charlie Hurt kicks me out on the street. There might even be enough left for a grocery run so I'm not stuck making Noah peanut butter sandwiches for the rest of the week.

But even with such happy thoughts to occupy me, I still can't get Cas out of my mind. It's almost like he's right next to me as I pocket the money. When I start washing glasses and wiping down the bar, I can still feel the rough scratch of his dark beard against my skin. I can see the patches of red that show when the sunlight hits it, and the deep brown of his eyes as they sought mine just before he kissed me. I can smell the masculine scent of him, all smoke and leather and the open road.

God, I *want* him. I sure as hell wish I didn't, but I do.

As the minutes tick by in the quiet bar, I start to get nervous at the thought of the meeting ending and having to face Cas again. Eventually, the heavy doors of the room they call the chapel finally open, and the men begin spilling out. I force myself not to look over and watch for him to exit with the others. Instead, I busy myself wiping the bar counter down, even though I just did that five minutes ago, and pretend I couldn't care less.

"Jenna, set us up with some shots," calls a man whose name I think is Brick. I do as he asks, pulling out a bottle of the whiskey these men seem to prefer and taking out some glasses. I'm thankful for the distraction, and don't even notice at first that Cas has come up to the bar and taken a seat at the other end.

"What can I get you?" I ask him casually when I walk over. My voice shakes just a little bit, but I'm hoping he doesn't notice.

"I'd take a replay of about an hour ago," he murmurs, his voice thick. And just like that, heat pools between my legs again, the throb returning. I don't know what to say to that, *at all*.

"You're pretty easy to please if you'd be satisfied with dry humping against a wall," I finally manage to toss off. I'm trying for bravado, but I don't really think I succeed.

"Oh, I'm not fucking satisfied. Not anywhere *near*." He chuckles low in his throat, and the sound is so dangerously sexy I'm instantly wet.

I don't say anything in return. Because I'm afraid that if I open my mouth, what will come out is, *Please please please fuck me*. So, I swallow once, painfully, and concentrate on the glass I'm drying like it's the most fascinating thing I've ever seen.

"How late we got you working tonight? What do you say we continue this conversation somewhere more private?" His voice is molten lava against my skin.

My nipples harden to pebbles as I imagine how it will feel when he slides his hands over my breasts. I suppress a shiver and feel my breath grow shallow.

Then I remember Noah.

"I don't have a sitter," I say slowly, trying to hide the deep disappointment I'm feeling.

Cas looks back toward the couch. "Just a second," he murmurs. Then, as I watch, he wanders over and has a brief conversation with Jewel. "Jewel's gonna take him," he tells me when he comes back. "Matter of fact, she says she'll be more than willing to babysit him whenever you need, since she can't tend bar."

I look over at Jewel, a question in my eyes, and she smiles and nods at me. Well, I guess my child care dilemma has been solved.

"I guess you've taken care of everything," I say slowly to Cas, my heart starting to pound in my chest.

His face widens into the maddeningly sexy grin I know only too well. "That's what I do. I take care of things." His eyes bore into mine. "And about three minutes after we leave this clubhouse, I'm going to take care of you."

Chapter 16

CAS

Thankfully, Jewel's hand isn't so bad that she can't drive a car. I ask Jenna for her keys, then tell Jewel where she lives and ask her to take Noah home and put him to bed.

Then I grab a beer from Jenna and wait for her to finish working so I can take her to my place.

Angel's hanging out at a table with Rock and a couple of the other men, so when it's almost time for Jenna to leave, I walk out first so he won't see us together. I'm sitting on the bike waiting when she comes out. She looks behind her at the front door as it closes behind her, like she's a spy or something afraid of being followed. I almost tease her about it, but frankly, my mind is on other things, and those things involve peeling off those shorts and plunging my tongue between her thighs. So I'm not in much of a joking mood.

Jenna doesn't seem to feel much like talking, either. Wordlessly, she gets on the bike behind me, not even asking where we're going. I don't have a helmet for her, so she quickly ties her hair in a ponytail and then wraps her arms around my torso. I feel her shiver ever so slightly. Blood flows to my dick in anticipation. I'm not sure how many times I've thought about my night with Jenna over the years, but it's been a lot. More than any other woman I've been with, for sure. The truth is, Jenna Abbott has *always* felt like unfinished business.

I told Jenna it would be three minutes after we left the bar that I'd be taking her. I'm not far off. I'm in my driveway with the engine off in five, and in six I've got her pushed up against my living room wall, shorts and panties at her ankles. Her breathing is coming in gasps, her legs trembling as I reach down and slide a finger inside her. She's soaking wet, so ready for me it's all I can do to not just bend her over the couch and fuck her right this second.

But I have other ideas. It's been almost five years since that night I spent with Jenna, and I'm not about to rush through this.

I slide my finger, slick with her juices, out of her and graze it softly across her puffy lower lips and already-hardening clit. She gasps and freezes, her head arching back. She's completely and utterly under my control, already. Her skin is on fire, so much so that my every touch speeds up and shallows her breathing. I bend down and close my mouth over hers, devouring her lips, and she moans into my mouth and kisses me back hungrily.

God fucking damn, she's hot.

I know I can make her come just like this, with my fingers, but that's not what I want. I continue to kiss her, stroking her clit again and chuckling deep in my throat as she tenses again and arches against my hand. With my other arm, I reach back and under and undo the clasp of her bra. Breaking away from her mouth, I pull the shirt over her head and fling the bra away, then take a step back to look at her. Jenna opens her eyes. Her blue eyes are dark, the pupils impossibly big. Her lips part, her heavy breathing making her breasts rise and fall rapidly.

Her fucking gorgeous breasts. They're just as lush and full as I remember them. More so. Her nipples are a little darker pink, a little larger than I remember them. There's a long, gold chain hanging down between them, with a ring on it, and a flash of recognition hits me: this is Jenna's mom's ring. She used to wear it back in the day, as well. I feel a pang of tenderness, remembering this. I gently take the necklace off over her head, laying it on a small table by the door so it doesn't break. Then I bend down and cup one luscious mound, flicking my tongue lightly over the taut bud.

Jenna throws back her head and lets out a loud moan. One hand comes up and fists in my hair, and she arches her breasts toward me, silently begging for more. My cock is harder than I ever remember it being. I continue to tease her, my hand going to the other nipple to graze it with my thumb.

Jenna's moans and cries are getting more desperate, and soon I'm sweeping her up in my arms and carrying her naked body through the hall to my bedroom.

Laying her down on the mattress, I throw off my cut, yank my T-shirt over my head and kick my jeans across the room. I allow myself one more glorious moment of staring at her fucking perfect body, her breasts rising and falling rapidly with her breathing. My hand goes to my thick cock to stroke it once, twice, but then I have to stop because I'm gonna lose control of myself if I don't.

Instead, I kneel down on the bed and push her knees apart. The beautiful sight of Jenna's pussy greets me, glistening and wet between her quivering thighs. Her breath hitches in her throat, her hips arching toward me. She knows what I'm about to do, and she wants it so bad she can hardly stand it. Even so, I take my time, slowly letting my breathing tease her inner thighs until she's whimpering in frustration. Then, finally, I push my tongue inside her, then lap slowly upwards until I've caressed her entire sex with my tongue.

Jenna shudders, and whispers something that might be a word. I could make her come in seconds, but I know I have to make it last for her. I lick and stroke at her folds, avoiding the most sensitive part, helping her climb higher and higher. She clutches at the sheets, her legs fall wider, her thighs tensing. I can feel from the motion of the mattress that her head is thrashing back and forth. The jewel of her clit is hard and pulsing, and finally, finally, when I know she can't take any more, I slide my lips over it and suck it gently into my mouth, worshiping it with my tongue as she cries out sharply and arches off the bed. Jenna shakes and bucks, and I hold her hips there and draw out her orgasm, licking her as she peaks again and again.

Finally, when she starts to quiet, I push myself up and grab my wallet from my jeans. I roll a condom onto my throbbing cock, then slide my head against the slick opening of her channel. My eyes roll shut. *Holy* fuck, *that's good.* I suppress a groan, knowing I'm not going to be able to slow myself down much. I need her *now*. I've waited long enough.

I push myself inside her, my jaw clenching against the pleasure. Jenna parts her lips and I hear her whisper. This time I can make it out: "Yes." I pull out, then press in again, deeper, until I'm completely inside. Slowly, as slowly as I can stand it, I start to move, thrusting exquisitely and trying to make it last as long as I can. Jenna moves with me, arching her hips to meet me, and soon my cock starts to swell, my balls heavy with seed. Then Jenna cries out again, shuddering, and it sends me over the edge. I empty myself deep inside her with a shout, the orgasm so intense I lose my breath for a second. I've told myself over the years that I'd exaggerated the memory of how good sex was with Jenna but I know now that I was wrong, it's *never* been like this with any other woman. Spasm after spasm rocks me, and when it's over I'm bracing myself on her thighs, almost dizzy from the force of it.

Jesus fuck.

That's when I make the decision: Jenna is staying here tonight. And I'm not letting her out of my sight until we do that again. And again.

Chapter 17

JENNA

I must have fallen asleep for a little bit, because when I wake up, it's to find Cas climbing back into bed with me.

"Ugh," I groan, stretching my arms out wide. "I should probably get going."

"Nope," he corrects me. "You're staying right here."

"Cas," I sigh. "I have to get back to Noah."

"Taken care of." He pulls up the covers and gathers me into his arms. "I just got off the phone with Jewel. She's more than happy to stay the night at your place with him."

"But I —"

"It's settled," he says firmly, interrupting me.

I open my mouth to protest again, but he gives me a look that's both stern and sexy, so I stop.

I shouldn't let Jewel do this, even though I'm sure she'll take good care of my son. I should get back to Noah.

But God, it's been *so* long since I've been able to feel like anything but a mom and, frankly, a cash-poor loser.

It's been so long since I've just felt like a *woman*. A sexy, desirable woman, even. And the way Cas Watkins looks at me, the way he touches me — I realize it's something I've been needing so much, for way, way too long.

With a sigh, I sink back against him and allow myself to close my eyes and luxuriate in the feeling. Just for a little while.

God, if only it could always be like this with a man.

Cas's hands begin to roam over me again now, and even though I thought I was completely exhausted, his touch reawakens my desire. He moves over me, then reaches for his jeans again, but I stop him.

This is crazy, I know. But I want it anyway.

"I'm on the pill," I breathe. "If you think you're clean."

I've been on the pill for years. Wishful thinking, mostly. It's not like I've actually *used* the protection. A hundred times, I've told myself I should just admit that I live in a sexual desert and stop refilling the prescription.

But right now I'm grateful for it. I want to feel Cas inside me. I want to *feel* us together, skin on skin.

"I don't do unprotected sex," he tells me. "I don't like surprises." I think that means he's refusing, but then he says, "So yeah, I'm clean." His eyes bore into mine, dark and stormy with desire. "You sure?"

The 'surprises' line hits me a little in the gut. Something must change in my expression, because Cas's face turns gentle.

"Look, if you're not sure, it's completely fine," he murmurs. "Don't do this just because you think I want it. Like I said, I'm not in the habit."

Shit. I feel like I'm wrecking this moment. "No," I say, reaching down for him. "I'm sure." My hand slides around his thick cock, gripping it. It's the first time I've actually *touched* him there. He feels *amazing*, the heft and weight of him making the rising ache between my legs even more painful. I'm dying to feel him inside me again.

Cas closes his eyes for a second as I begin to slowly stroke him. "Fuck," he hisses. "You've got me on the goddamn edge already, Jen." I angle my hips upward, and he presses the thick head of his shaft against my opening. Closing my eyes, I exhale slowly as he joins us together, skin to skin. God, the *heat* of him inside me like this… it's unbelievable. He's perfect, it's all so perfect, that for a second I just freeze and marvel at what it feels like to have him inside me, filling me so completely.

We begin to move, a rhythm that starts out slow but quickly becomes more driven, more frenetic. I can feel the two of us begin to climb higher and higher together, Cas's moans joining with mine. Our bodies *need* this, with an urgency I can tell is the same for both of us.

"Cas," I moan.

"I know, baby," he croons at me. "I know. Come with me, baby."

"Oh, God, I'm so close. Oh, Cas, please don't stop, I'm… Oh God YES!"

I shatter just as he empties himself inside me with a roar, our bodies shuddering together. For a few moments, I sort of lose all sense of my body's borders, like my body is Cas's body and both of us have expanded out into the universe. When I finally start coming back to my senses, Cas is kissing me deeply, our bodies entwined, with him still inside me.

He's whispering things about how gorgeous I am, and how sexy I am, and for a few minutes, I just feel so incredibly *happy* — like seriously, probably the happiest I've ever felt in my whole life. The only thing that comes close is the day I gave birth to Noah, but even that happiness was ringed with fear and worry and *oh my God how in the hell am I qualified to be somebody's mother?* But this… right now… is just *bliss*.

The sex, of course, is amazing. Sex with Cas is so much better than it's ever been with anyone else that I'm a little worried he might have ruined me for future boyfriends —

assuming I ever manage to have a boyfriend again. But it's more than that. What just happened between us feels… *intimate*. It feels like it was more than just sex, more than just *fucking*.

It's not, though. I know better than to let myself imagine things that aren't there. I'm probably just so sex-starved after all this time that I'm imagining things.

But he did ask me to stay the night. Practically insisted on it.

Stop it, Jenna. Stop reading into it. Cas could have any woman he wanted to, practically. Just because he's choosing me tonight doesn't mean anything. I need to just enjoy it for what it is: a much-needed vacation from reality.

Chapter 18
Jenna

I should be exhausted after our second round of sex, but for some reason I'm wide awake afterwards. Luckily, Cas seems like he isn't in any hurry to go to sleep, either. We fall into an easy rhythm of conversation, catching up with what we've each been doing for the past few years — as though we're not lying in bed naked next to one another after two rounds of mind-blowing sex.

I tell him about going back to school for a second year of college, and then dropping out again. What I *don't* tell him is why. That after I'd discovered I was pregnant, I made it through the school year, and even Noah's birth, but in the end I couldn't make it all work financially with a baby on a full-time student's budget.

I feel a twinge of guilt and nerves as I tell him all this. Part of me is both hoping and dreading that he'll put two and two together and figure out that Noah is his. I should tell him, I know. Now that Cas has actually *met* Noah, I feel like I *have* to tell him. But how do you do that? How do you tell a guy, "Hey, by the way, that kid running around with deep brown eyes and a shock of brown hair? Yeah, he's yours. Sorry I forgot to tell you at the time."

The fact is, I agonized about whether to tell Cas about Noah throughout the entire pregnancy. But I didn't want him to think I was trying to rope him into a relationship. And I didn't want Noah to have a father who didn't want him. In the end, I told myself that I could love my son enough for two parents. But it was easier to believe that when he was a baby. Now that he's older, I know Noah is starting to miss having a father. And now that I'm back in Tanner Springs, it's even harder to figure out how to navigate all this.

Especially since here I am back in Cas's bed.

"Hey," Cas is saying, as he begins to twine a lock of my hair around his finger. "What's with the hair, by the way?"

"What do you mean?" I ask.

"Why did you dye it?"

Oh. I've been coloring my hair for a while now. Long enough that I forgot Cas hasn't ever seen me as a brunette before. "I don't know," I shrug. "I guess… I thought people would take me more seriously as a brunette. You'd be surprised how many people seem to believe the 'dumb blonde' thing."

"Huh." He's quiet for a moment.

"What?" Now I'm self-conscious. Reaching up to touch my head, I ask, "Does it look bad?"

"No, no. Not at all." He looks at me. "It looks good, actually. It's hot. But…" For a couple of seconds he looks like he's trying to decide what to say. Finally, he murmurs, "I get that it's just hair, Jen. Women dye their hair all the time. But… don't cover yourself up, okay?" His face is serious. "You don't need to hide from anyone. Be yourself."

Anger flashes through me. I *hate* when guys tell women how to dress, or how much makeup they should have on, or how to do their hair. It happens to me all the damn time. I open my mouth to tell Cas to go to hell, but then I close it again.

Because as pissed off as part of me is that he thinks he should get to tell me what to do with my hair…

He's right.

I dye my hair *precisely* to cover myself up. To hide the part of me that does nothing but screw things up. To look more serious, more capable.

But for the first time, I realize that I'm not hiding myself from other people. I'm hiding myself from myself.

And somehow, Cas Watkins saw right through me.

I'm not about to let him know that, though.

"What about you?" I challenge. "You're hiding behind that big bad biker thing." I'm trying to rile him up — suddenly I want him to be angry with me — but he just laughs.

"I'm not hiding anything, Jen." He lifts his head to grin suggestively at me. "What you see is what you get. And you've *seen* pretty much everything."

I blush. "That's not what I mean, and you know it." I wave my hands around. "You're Big, Bad, mysterious Ghost Watkins, Sergeant at Arms for the Lords of Carnage. You're trying to tell me that's not something you use to keep the world at a distance?"

He shrugs. Clearly, I'm not getting under his skin as much as I want to. "Not more than anyone else," he says calmly. "The club's a brotherhood. I'm not hiding from anything."

I snort. "I don't buy it."

"What would I be hiding?" he asks, raising his hands wide.

"I don't know. You tell me," I say. "I mean, I barely know anything about you. How would I know what you're hiding?"

"What do you mean?" He frowns, genuinely perplexed. "We've known each other for years."

"Yeah, but… what do we really *know* about each other?" I persist.

"I know what makes you scream," he says reaching for me.

"Stop!" I bat him away. "I'm serious."

"Okay, okay," he laughs. "What do you want to know?"

"Ummm…" I sit for a few seconds, thinking. "Okay. Cats or dogs?"

"What?" He's confused.

"Which do you like better?" I explain. "Cats or dogs?"

"Oh." He cocks his head at me. The smirk on his face tells me he's considering whether to play this silly game with me. Finally, he relents. "Dogs. You?"

"Both," I say. "With a slight preference for dogs. Okay, now your turn."

"Are we seriously doing this?" he complains, but I'm not having it.

"Yes. Your turn. Go."

He sighs dramatically. "Okay. Uh. Day or night?"

"Hm. Day," I smile. "I love the sunshine on my face. You?"

"Night," he grins, reaching out to stroke my breast. I shiver, but push him away. "Pizza or hamburgers?"

"You have to choose between pizza and hamburgers?" I ask.

"This is your game," he reminds me.

"Pizza. As long as I can have different flavors." I specify. "Okay, my turn." I think for a second. "Leather or lace?"

"What? On me?" He starts laughing.

"No, silly. On women." I shrug my shoulders. "Like, do you like women who wear jeans and leather, or more frilly, girly stuff?"

"Whatever you're wearing is good with me," he growls. "Right now I'm partial to naked."

"Focus," I say. "Oh, here's a good one. Movies or books?"

"Books," he replies firmly.

"Seriously?"

"What?" he protests. "You think I can't read?"

"No, no, it's just… a little hard to imagine you reading." I admit, eyeing him curiously. "What's your favorite book?"

"*The Count of Monte Cristo*," he replies instantly. "My granddad gave it to me when I was a kid. I still have it. And you've asked like three questions in a row."

"Okay, sorry. Your turn."

He looks at me for a few seconds, thinking. Then finally: "Regret something you have done, or regret something you haven't done?"

Whoa. I thought this was just a stupid game. But once again, it's like somehow Cas has just reached inside my head.

Regretting things has become almost a religion for me. I've made so many stupid mistakes in my life so far. Sometimes I think making mistakes is all I'm good at.

I almost just give him a flippant answer so we can move on. But instead, I can't help but turn Cas's question over in my head. I think about my fling with him all those years ago. It's a fling I regretted almost instantly. But it gave me Noah. I can't regret that, no matter what.

I don't know what's going on between Cas and me, now, either. It might end up blowing up in my face. But if I'm honest with myself? I can't regret this, either, no matter what happens.

The one thing I really, *really* regret as I sit here right now, though? That I never told Cas about Noah. That I'm going to have to do it eventually, and it's probably going to be way worse because I didn't do it when I should have.

"I'd rather regret something I had done," I finally choke out.

"Me, too," he breathes, bending toward me. He kisses me, deeply, and then for the third time in a night — just like our first night together — we come together, crying out our passion in the dark.

Afterwards, we lie panting next to each other.

"I sure as hell don't regret *that*," Cas murmurs.

I burst out laughing.

Chapter 19

CAS

I manage to see Jenna most nights for the next couple of weeks. It's not like I plan it that way. It just sort of happens. Whenever she's in my arms, she's all I can think about. And whenever I'm away from her, all I can think about is seeing her again.

Usually, I come over to her place at night. Most of the time it's after Noah's gone to bed, but sometimes when I get there he's still up, all fed and bathed and in his pajamas. I've never paid a hell of a lot of attention to little kids, but I gotta say that Noah's a pistol. Smart as a damn whip, too. He's already reading, even though he's not even in kindergarten yet. Jenna told me he just figured it out one day. I guess she was reading a book to him and he interrupted her and started sounding the words out himself. He even brought me one of his little books one night and read it to me out loud, sitting next to me on Jenna's old worn-out couch with his stuffed monkey beside him. He's always asking questions about how things work, and he's got this damn quirky sense of humor, too. He cracks me up, which is pretty damn amazing in a four-year-old. It's weird — in some ways, the kid really reminds me of me.

In normal circumstances, I would have run as fast as I could away from a chick with a kid. Hell, the last thing I need is some woman looking for a daddy figure in her rug rat's life. But Jenna's not like that. At all. She's not forcing Noah on me. Just the opposite, in fact. Which is why I'm surprised to realize I'm actually *enjoying* spending time with him.

Being with Jenna has this weird… *thing* about it. This weird quality. It's like, every time I'm with her, it feels familiar and new at the same time. It's exciting as hell — and Jesus Christ, the sex is *scorching* hot — but it's also sort of more *there* than with other women I've been with. It's like every time I kiss her or touch her, I get to have the memory of how it felt the first time — plus all the years in between when I would think about her in odd moments and feel this little pull and twinge of regret — plus *now* when she's older and hotter and holy shit *amazing* at sex. A few days ago she gave me a blow job, and when I came I thought my brain was gonna blow out the back of my head.

It's sort of like I've been missing her this whole time and didn't even know it, until she showed up.

And the thought of her eventually packing up again and moving on makes something constrict painfully in my throat.

Things start to fall into a sort of routine with us. A nice one, though. Jenna takes Noah to Jewel's place every day to be babysat, and I see her at night, when we're both away from the clubhouse. Of course, I see her during the day, too, when she's working at the bar. But we're keeping whatever this is private for now, especially because Angel will probably lose his shit if he finds out about us.

The sneaking around thing is kind of fun at first, but it gets old really fucking fast.

One afternoon, I'm at the clubhouse while Jenna's working. I'd kept her up pretty damn late the night before, and even though she looks a little tired, she's goddamn beautiful and sexy as hell. I'm having a hard time not going behind the bar and pulling her against my cock, which I'm fighting to keep under control. I settle for shooting her the occasional dirty glance, smiling to myself when she blushes and starts to squirm.

I nonchalantly wander over just as she's serving Gunner a drink. He's ordered his typical, a Jack and coke spiked with vodka. Jenna sets the glass in front of him and then turns to me saucily, the hint of a blush flushing her cheeks.

"What'll you have?" she asks me saucily, her eyes daring me to say something dirty.

"Hey, what is this?" Gunner complains. "This ain't vodka, it's gin!"

"Shit! Sorry," Jenna stammers. She takes the glass from him and pours it out. "I guess I'm just a little distracted today."

"No worries, darlin'," Gunner replies, giving her a grin and a wink. "You can pay me back later."

"You wish," Jenna shoots back easily. I'll give it to her, she can definitely hold her own around these animals.

Jenna redoes Gunner's drink and hands it to him. He moves away, and I lean closer and murmur, "I'll have a tall glass of Jenna Abbott."

Jenna looks away and smothers a smile. "Stop it! You're being too distracting. It's your fault I messed up Gunner's drink in the first place."

"Oh, sure, blame it on me."

"It's true!" She lowers her voice. "I can't get last night out of my head with you staring at me like that. You make me feel naked."

"Your mouth to God's ears," I mutter. "When do you get off, anyway? So I can *get you* off."

"Filthy," she says.

"You know it."

A couple of the other brothers come up and ask for bottles of beer. "Hey, sweet stuff," Hawk drawls, "How'd you like to join me later for a little extra-curricular activity?"

"Sorry, Hawk. I've got to pick up my *son*." She stresses the word for good measure.

"Rain check, then," he says, undeterred. He stares off into space, a lecherous gleam in his eye. "I've always wondered what it would be like with a MILF."

A couple of the other brothers murmur their approval, and one makes a rude noise. Easy laughter bubbles up from Jenna's throat.

"Same as with anyone else," she says. "Just with more sleep deprivation."

Jenna gets a lot of this kind of ribbing from the brothers while she's working. It's mostly good natured — after all, she is the VP's sister — but every single one of them would fuck her in a heartbeat, I know. Jenna takes it in stride, but after a while it starts to piss me the hell off that she has to flirt with the rest of those assholes just to make tips. She's not doing a damn thing wrong, but I find myself wanting to stand up and beat my fucking chest or something for dominance. Yell out to everyone in the bar, "Hands off, goddamnit. Jenna's mine. *Mine*."

I've never really had anything resembling a relationship with a woman before. The most you could say is that I've fucked a few more than once. But I've never been one for half-measures. No one else is going to have Jenna Abbott. Because she's mine. Body and soul. *Jenna belongs to me.* The words resound in my mind, persistent as a heartbeat. The club might not know it yet, but they will. And I'm gonna make sure Jenna knows it, as well.

Chapter 20

JENNA

Cas slips behind the bar with me when most of the men are in the back room playing pool. "You're coming with me after your shift," he murmurs in my ear. His hot breath tickles my skin, and my eyes flutter closed as a flame lights low in my belly.

"Cas, be careful," I whisper. "What if someone sees you?"

"I don't fucking care," he growls. There's something up with him today: a tension and urgency in his body that I can feel as he leans into me. Between my legs, a familiar ache begins to grow, as it always does when he gets this close to me. His cock is hardening as he presses against my ass. *Oh, God...* We've been together long enough now that I know exactly what he can do to me, and *exactly* how good it's going to feel when he does...

"I'll call Jewel and see if she can keep Noah a little later," I say in a strangled voice. Then I slide away from him before I burst into flames. He moves away to the other side of the bar, and I exhale in relief. Being around that man is dangerous when I have to pretend there's nothing going on between us.

There's not a whole lot going on at the clubhouse today, so I have a little more time to myself just to think and enjoy the relatively slow pace. It's funny, but even though I have to put up with the men flirting with me, I actually sort of *like* working here. It's nice to feel like I belong, for once. Since I'm Angel's sister, I'm off limits, so I know I don't have to take any of their B.S.'ing seriously. I get to watch from an amused distance as the fully-patched members test out the prospects, making them do their grunt work to see whether they'll be loyal to the club. I've even struck up friendships with some of the old ladies. For maybe the first time in my life, I don't feel like I'm "less than," or like I'm not living up to anyone's expectations. I just feel like I fit in. It's a welcome relief from being around my father, who always seems to be disappointed in me and my choices.

My father... I breathe out a sigh as my thoughts turn to him. I've been kind of avoiding Dad the last couple of weeks, mostly because I don't want to deal with his prying questions about what my future plans are. He knows I'm working at the clubhouse now, and I'm pretty sure he doesn't approve —

though when I told him, he didn't blow up like I thought he would. In fact, he was downright subdued about it, to the point where I almost asked him why he wasn't more upset. *Something's bothering him,* I think. And it seems like whatever it is goes deeper than just the reelection campaign.

My hand goes up to finger my mom's ring as I think guiltily about the three voicemails I have on my cell phone from him. *I really need to call him back one of these days,* I tell myself. He does deserve at least that much. After all, it's because of him that I have a roof over my head. Even though I'm doing a lot better financially now, and soon I'll be able to pay him back for the damage deposit, I should probably make a point to thank him again for helping me in the first place. I resolve to be a better daughter to my dad. Heck, maybe I'll even bring Noah over to see him for an hour or two this weekend.

My thoughts continue to ping-pong back and forth between turning over a new leaf with my dad and wondering what Cas has planned for us after I'm done working. I call Jewel and make sure she's okay with taking Noah for a couple more hours. Somehow, I manage to make it through the rest of my shift. Then I drive home to take a quick shower, because I spilled beer on myself earlier, and really, that's just not a sexy smell.

Cas shows up at my place about ten minutes after I get out of the shower. My hair's still wet, and I feel a little self-conscious that I haven't had time to dry it and put a little makeup on. But when he strides through my door and pulls me to him like I'm a glass of water and he's dying of thirst, my disheveled state doesn't seem to matter so much.

"God damn, I thought I was gonna go crazy back at the bar," he murmurs in my ear. One hand goes around the back of my neck, the other to my hip, pulling me hard against him. He's already huge with need. His lips come crashing down on mine, his mouth taking me, possessing me. I make a small sound between a gasp and a moan as I open to him.

My hips are pressing against him, the ache between my legs already almost unbearable. Cas's urgency is contagious. I want him — I want *this* — *now*. My feverish hands go to his waistband and start to fumble open his fly.

"No," he growls, grabbing my arm. "Not here."

I catch a ragged breath and try to focus on what he's saying. "Where, then?" I'm confused. I can't see why he'd rather take the time to go to his place. It's not that much different from mine, other than it's nicer, and has a larger bed.

But apparently he's determined. "Come with me," he rasps. He hasn't let go of my wrist, and starts to pull me out the front door.

"Uh, Cas?" I begin, pulling back on my arm and halting in my tracks.

"Yeah?" He bites the word out, clearly impatient.

"Maybe I should — you know — put some clothes on first?"

For the first time, he seems to notice that I'm only wearing an oversized T-shirt.

"Oh. Yeah," he mutters. "Well, okay. Hurry up."

His tone is gruff, but I know it's not anger — at least, not at me. Still, I don't waste any time. I go into my tiny bedroom and stare at the closet. I consider what to wear for a moment, but then tell myself that wherever it is that Cas is taking me, it's likely I won't be wearing clothes for very long.

In the end I just pull on a pair of jeans and a tank top, then pull my hair into a pony and walk back out in to the main room. Cas is already standing impatiently at the front door, and pushes it open to let me go through.

Outside, the air's already starting to cool, the sun about halfway down its descent to the horizon. Cas gets on the bike and I climb on behind him. I take a moment to breathe in deeply and relish the solid warmth of him — the deep comfort and masculinity of a powerful man on a powerful bike.

I wrap my arms around his waist and snuggle close. Then he fires up the engine and we drive out into the evening, leaving Tanner Springs behind.

Chapter 21

JENNA

It's been so long that I've forgotten all about this place. I can't figure out where he's taking me until we're practically there. But when he takes the last turn onto the dirt road, something snaps into place in my head. I start to laugh against his chest, the sound drowned out by the engine.

"Why are you laughing?" he growls as he looks back at me, but his eyes are twinkling.

"You're seriously taking me to this run-down old place?" I call out, my tone teasing.

But I don't mean it. Not at *all*.

It's the old motor home. The place Cas took me that first night, all those years ago.

Cas pulls in and cuts the engine. "What do you mean, run-down?" he protests. "This place is fucking classy."

Cas waits for me to hop off the bike, then pulls it up on the stand and gets off himself. To be fair, it *does* look a lot better than I remember it being. The tall grass around the motor home has been mowed into a sort of yard, and the door that Cas busted off its hinges to get in has been repaired.

"Donnie fixed the place up a year or so ago," he says, producing a key and unlocking the door. He gestures ceremoniously for me to enter. "I'd carry you in," he tells me, "but I'm pretty sure there's no way we're fitting through this door together."

Inside, the place is recognizable, but a lot cleaner and a lot more modern. It still has some of the musty odor I remember, but it's less rough. It's almost… *homey*, in a way. I mean, it's no Better Homes and Gardens, but it's a lot better than it used to be.

"Donnie never figured out who busted in back then," Cas chuckles. "I finally told him it was me a couple years ago. He chewed my ass for it."

"I bet he did," I smile. "But how did you get a key? Did he give you one?"

"Yeah," Cas grins. "I guess he thought it'd be better than having me busting his door open again."

"Good point," I snort. I spend a few seconds looking around. "This place isn't bad. You could almost live here."

"Yeah, depending on how much you wanted to rough it. There's still no electricity." Cas opens a cupboard and takes out a bunch of candles in simple holders. One by one, he lights them with his lighter and sets them on various surfaces, until the room is bathed in a warm, golden light.

It's... *romantic*.

Or, I'm just a sucker for weird, dark, smelly trailers.

"So, you bring many of your conquests out here?" I joke, turning towards him. I expect Cas to laugh, but he freezes, suddenly serious.

"No," he says simply. "I've never brought anyone else out here."

Something in his tone makes me feel like... apologizing? "It was kind of a joke," I stammer, feeling kind of lame. I mean, I'll grant you, the thought of him bringing someone out here does make me feel a little jealous. But I wasn't fishing for a denial. After all, we both have pasts. In fact, we both have almost five years of pasts since we last saw each other. A man like Cas, I know, has probably had more women than he can count in that time.

Unlike me. I can count the men I've been with since Cas on exactly one finger.

Being a single mom of a young son will do that to you.

Cas pulls me tightly into his arms. His length presses hard against me. "Jen." His voice goes low and raspy. "I've never brought anyone else out here but you. And not just here. Anywhere, really. You're the only woman I've ever wanted to have memories with. A past." He pauses. "And a future."

Cas is so serious all of a sudden... and he's almost never serious. I can't think of anything to say, but luckily, Cas takes care of that for me by lowering his mouth to mine. His lips are demanding, devouring me. His tongue swirls against mine, tasting, possessing, until I'm feeling dizzy. I cling to him, feeling the heat begin to pool between my legs. God, it's so good with him. I'm afraid of getting used to this, but that's just exactly what's happening.

He grins sexily at me now, his eyes flashing in the candlelight. "I still remember how sexy you were that night. Goddamn sexiest thing I'd ever seen. You were a fucking fantasy, you know that?"

"Were?" I manage to tease.

"Are." His lips are hard against mine, his hand holding my head fast. His tongue winds around mine, claiming it, and I let out a little moan and sing into the kiss, my heart pounding fast. After a moment, Cas pulls back, and growls almost angrily, "Fuck, you still are, Jenna. You're in my head all the time. You know how goddamn crazy it makes me to see how all the men at the club want you? You know how bad I want to claim you? To tell them to keep their fucking hands off you and their dicks in their pants?"

The hand that was behind my head slips down to pull my hips against his, the other one sliding up to my breast. My breath hitches in my throat. "You're mine, Jenna," he mutters. "All fucking mine." His hand moves under my shirt, under my bra, and he grazes my sensitive nipple with his thumb. I suppress a moan. "Tell me you're mine," he insists.

"I'm…" I gasp. "I'm yours."

"Your body is mine," he growls. "I'm the only one that gets to touch you like this."

"The only one," I repeat obediently, shuddering at his touch.

"I'm the only one that gets to make you come." He presses my sex harder against him, and my eyes flutter closed as I grind my hips against him, already desperate to relieve the ache. "Tell me," he demands.

"Yes," I breathe, but it comes out like I'm begging. "Yes, God, Cas…"

He pulls me down onto the bed, so I'm straddling him, and as he pulls off my tank top and my bra I'm yanking his T-shirt over his head. I move my hips along his length, and God, it feels so *good*. His hands run roughly over my skin, cupping my breasts and beginning to pinch my nipples just hard enough to make me briefly wonder if I'm going to come just like that. I can't wait, can't stand much more, and when his mouth closes over one of the areolas I make a noise deep in my throat that's almost animal. He swirls his tongue around it, then closes soft lips over it and begins to suck gently as his thumb teases my other nipple. I'm practically writhing against his cock now, my fingers digging into his shoulders for leverage. My body has taken over, my mind's no longer even in control of what I'm doing, the only thought in my brain is *now now now make me come now oh god…*

Suddenly, Cas breaks away with a groan. "You're gonna make me lose all control like that," he rasps, and grabs my ass to set me aside. I watch as he kicks off his jeans and sets his thick shaft free. My mouth actually *waters* as I shimmy my jeans off as well, my eyes never leaving him. Mesmerized, I reach out and wrap my hand around him, stroking the hot, velvety skin and moving forward to take him in my mouth.

Cas hisses as my lips wrap around the large head. His skin is taut, and I love the way it feels against my tongue as I lick and stroke it. His fingers fist in my hair, guiding me as I slide him in and out, but I know he won't let me keep doing this for long. I can tell just by the way he's restraining himself. Sure enough, about thirty seconds later he pulls himself away from me, ignoring my moan of protest. Then before I even realize what's happening, I'm on my back, and he's on his knees in front of me.

"Jesus Christ," Cas groans as his head slicks against my soaking lower lips. "You're so fucking wet for me, Jenna. You're wet for *me*."

"Yes," I tell him. "For your cock." I never talked dirty before, but with Cas there's just something about his cock that makes me want to *call* it that. It's so massive, so huge. It is a *cock*, if ever there was one. He's sliding the head along my pussy lips, gliding it around my clit, and my thighs tense as I angle my hips toward him. It feels fucking *amazing*, the heat of his skin against my wetness like that. I'm wound up tight as a rubber band, and I know he knows it. "Cas," I urge him, and bite my lip, waiting for him to free me from the exquisite torture. "Please… I need it… Oh, God, I need you right now, just like this…"

A low noise, almost like he's in pain, comes from deep in his throat as I strain toward him. Then, finally, he shifts on his knees and slams deep inside me, the top of his shaft sliding against my sensitive nub. *Oh, God, yes!* I'm so wet I coat the length of him, so when he pulls out and slides in again, it's slick and perfect and delicious, and he rides me, watching me as I arch my back, *hard*, and shatter, my channel clutching him. Cas pulls back and drives himself into me, harder, harder, filling me with his cock and prolonging my orgasm as I call out his name. Then, I literally *feel* him get larger inside me, and he tenses and explodes, filling me with white-hot heat as the pleasure rockets through me.

"You're mine," he whispers against my ear as he holds me to him.

"I'm yours," I whisper back.

Chapter 22

CAS

"I'm yours," she whispered, trembling in my arms.

Her words are still echoing in my head the next day. Last night was... well, fuck. It was incredible. I still can't quite believe that Jenna's back in my life, let alone that I want her — or any woman, for that matter — to *stay* in my life.

But one look at Jenna's body, full and lush in the candlelight, and it's not only lust I feel. It's goddamn *reverence*. My throat almost closes up with the beauty of her. As she came shuddering in my arms, and I released myself deep inside her, all I could think about was how I couldn't imagine not having Jenna in my life. I'd never even considered what it would be like to spend my life with a woman before. But last night, as she fell asleep in my arms, my mind was reeling with how much I'd changed in just a short time. Because of her. Because of this. Because of how *right* it all felt.

I'm still thinking about all of it as I walk out of another tense club meeting with Angel today. Rock brought another proposal to the table for the club to consider. Apparently, Abe Abbott is looking for a loan, to finance his stalled development project on the south side of town, and he came to Rock to find out if the club was willing to front him the cash.

"Why's he coming to us for this?" Skid barked, his face a mask of suspicion.

"Probably because the bank won't help him," I said. "Pretty damn bad news if a bank won't cough up a loan for the mayor." Next to me, Gunner snorted.

"How the fuck are we gonna give him a loan when we don't have enough cash to even pay ourselves?" Brick complained. "Makes no damn sense."

"We got enough to do this," Rock cut in. "We can get it, anyway."

"I dunno," I said, shaking my head. "There's been a lot of rival MC activity out there from the Iron Spiders. Seems like we could spend a lot of goddamn time and effort protecting our assets if we get involved in this shit." I looked around the table to see a few of the brothers nodding.

"We can handle it," Rock growled. "The fuckin' Spiders aren't gonna stop me from doin' what I want."

"You mean what the *club* wants," Brick corrected him pointedly. "And that's assuming we want it."

Rock's face was dark as he turned to face Brick. "Yeah. What the club wants. But you fuckers have been bellyaching about new ways to make money. Well, this is what I got. And Ghost is right. If Abbott's coming to us on this, it means the banks won't touch him. And him coming to us means we can charge him high interest, and demand a cut of the profits from the development. It'd be steady, real money for a long, long time."

Things started heating up between the brothers who thought this was a good idea and the ones who wanted nothing to do with it, but still wanted money. Eventually, things got so rough that Angel called for a break, so everyone could calm the hell down before we put it to a vote.

The two of us are standing outside in the parking lot now, having a smoke and talking about the deal before we go back into chapel.

"I dunno, man," Angel's saying. "Rock's talked to me about it a lot in the last couple days, and he keeps telling me it's a sure thing. The way he talks about it, it makes a hell of a lot of sense. But just the fact of how hard he's pushing makes me think he's trying to convince himself of that. He's got dollar signs in his eyes. I'm kind of on the fence."

"Look, I wanna say something," I begin. "But I'm not sure if I'm talking to my VP or my friend here. Or to Abe Abbott's son."

Angel cocks his head and frowns. "C'mon, Ghost. You know we're friends first. More than that. We're brothers. Family."

Family. Angel doesn't know the half of it. For a moment, I realize how accurate that actually is, now that I'm with Jenna. But now's not the time to bring that up, of course.

A kernel of guilt starts to grow inside me, but I push it down quickly. When Jenna's ready, we'll tell Angel about us. And I'll take whatever he needs to say or do to me. But for now, I have no choice but to keep it from him.

"Okay," I nod. "Look, this whole thing smells bad to me. Most everyone pushing for this deal has some reason for it that's clouding their minds. Rock wants money. Your dad, well I'm guessing he wants a big something to show the community so he'll win reelection easily against that Holloway asshole." I took a drag on my smoke. "If you vote in favor, your dad and Rock are gonna love you. And you're gonna be taking heat from both sides if you oppose it. Hell, you're going to be taking heat on this either way."

"But you think I should," Angel says, finishing my thought. "Oppose it, I mean."

"Yeah. I think you should." I nod slowly. "But it ain't gonna be easy."

We finish our cigarettes and head back inside for the vote. When we're all seated and Rock has called us back to order, we do one final round of discussion. A few of the men take the floor and say they're in favor of the deal with Abbott. Finally, Angel asks to speak.

"It's too risky," he says bluntly. "We're spread too thin. And like Ghost said, the Spiders' activity in that area makes me suspicious." I glance over at Rock while Angel's talking, and see him staring daggers at my friend.

"Of course you'd say that," Brick explodes. "You're a goddamn rich boy. You're the son of the mayor. You've never had to hustle for money."

"Fuck you, brother," Angel barks, rounding on him. "This fucking *club* is my family. My father can go fuck himself."

"Why the hell would Angel be against this deal if he was loyal to the mayor, Brick?" Gunner challenges him. "You're talking shit."

"If you're so goddamn loyal to this club, then why don't you make a decision that actually *benefits* the club?" Hawk shouts, half-rising from his chair.

"It's not gonna benefit the club if this deal takes us down," I say quietly.

The argument heats up, to the point that I think it might even come to blows here in the chapel. But before it does, Rock bangs loudly on the table with his gavel.

"Okay, enough," roars Rock angrily. "Enough. Let's just put this to a vote and make a decision."

One by one, we go around the table. In the end, Angel casts the deciding vote.

Nay.

The deal falls through.

"Good luck, brother," I mutter to him as we leave the chapel, angry silence surrounding us. "Being VP is gonna be a rough road for a while."

"Yeah," he says glumly. If I *stay* VP."

Chapter 23

JENNA

"Mommy!"

Noah opens the door just as I'm coming down the hall to Jewel's apartment. He runs up to me, his face all sticky with what looks like grape jam. "Jewel let me make my sandwich all by myself!"

As we reach the apartment, Jewel appears in the doorway. She smiles indulgently down at my son and then looks at me. "He did a great job spreading the peanut butter and jelly. He even managed to cut it into squares." Her eyes twinkle. "Well, more or less squares. More like… what are those things? Trapezoids?"

I laugh. "I get the picture."

Jewel motions for me to come inside. "Watch the doorknob, though," she warns me. "I have a feeling there's peanut butter on it."

Noah runs back inside, and I follow him into Jewel's small, tidy apartment. As always, I'm struck by how little this looks like the space lived in by an MC club bartender. *Well, you're one, too,* I remind myself. *People would probably find you just as unusual.*

"Have a seat," Jewel tells me. "You want anything to drink? I've got iced tea. It's so hot today."

It is indeed. Jewel's got her windows wide open to try to cool her place off. There's one small window air conditioner in the living room, but she's told me it doesn't work, and her landlord doesn't seem particularly interested in fixing it.

I sit down on her tiny love seat. Jewel calls Noah into the kitchen and I watch as she wipes off his hands and face with a wet cloth. He puts up with the cleaning impatiently, then runs over to me and bounces onto the love seat next to me.

"It looks like you and Jewel had a good day today, bug," I say to him.

"Yeah! She even drawed dinosaurs for me and I colored them in!" he beams. "I made one that was you, one that was Jewel, and one that was me!"

"Wow, so I'm a dinosaur now?" I tease him.

"No!" he crows, rolling his eyes. "You're a mommy!"

Jewel comes into the room with two glasses, and hands one to me.

"Thanks for being so great with him, Jewel," I say as she sits down. Noah wiggles down off the couch, presumably to go get his dinosaur drawings. "I honestly don't know what I would have done without you these last few weeks."

"No worries at all," she assures me. She pulls her hair back from her face with her uninjured hand. "He really is a darling." She looks back at him with a smile. "Like I told you, he kind of reminds me of my little brother." She looks sad for a moment, and I find myself wondering what kind of life she left behind in Indiana, and how she ended up here.

Jewel blinks then, and her face changes back to the bright, sunny smile she usually wears.

I pull my wallet out of my purse, then count out some bills and hand them to her.

"Thanks," she smiles. "Noah seems pretty excited for preschool."

It's Friday, and the last day Jewel will be watching Noah full-time. He's starting preschool on Monday, so she'll only be taking him a couple of afternoons a week while I'm at work.

I sigh nervously.

"I sure hope his excitement lasts," I say. "He seemed to like it when we went for a visit, anyway. And I think he's going to like his teachers."

"It must be strange, sending him to school for the first time," she remarks.

"It is," I admit. "But he's ready. And he needs some friends. I've been dragging him around from place to place for too long. He needs some stability in his life." My heart constricts as I think about all I've had to put my little boy through in his short life.

"How's your hand, by the way?" I ask, nodding toward the bandage, which I notice is smaller today.

"It's okay. I mean, it's healing fine." She shrugs. "I figure it'll still be a couple weeks until I'll be able to go back to tending bar." She sighs. "I can't *wait* to be able to take a normal shower without having to put a bag around my hand to keep the water out."

"Gosh, I'll bet." Noah comes back, his outstretched hands proudly displaying his artwork. The dinosaur version of me is purple, with a long neck, tiny arms and a huge body.

I try not to take it personally.

"Wow, those are pretty, Noah," I say, admiring.

"Look!" he says proudly, holding out one of the sheets. "I made one of Cas, too!"

It's a fourth sheet of paper, with an outline by Jewel of a large, strong-looking dinosaur. Noah has colored it a deep blue.

I glance quickly up at Jewel, searching her face for any reaction. "Noah asked me to draw one for him, as well. He said he was going to give it to Cas the next time he came over to your place," she says hesitantly.

She's trying not to react, but it's as plain as day that she knows what's going on between Cas and me. *Of course she does.* Jewel and I have never talked about Cas one way or another, but I realize now how much Cas and I have taken her secrecy for granted.

Reddening, I take the picture from Noah. "Uh, that's really nice, Noah. I think Cas will really like it. Now why don't you go get your stuff ready, okay, bug?"

He runs off to collect his things. When he's gone, Jewel gives me a kind look. "He's a good guy, Cas is," she says simply. "Any girl would be lucky to have him."

I freeze at first, afraid to say anything. But it seems silly to deny that there's something going on between us. Jewel already knows, and lying to her face just seems wrong when she's been taking care of Noah so that we could be together.

"When I first started tending bar for the club," she continues, "The guys were a little… rough. Before this job, I used to be a stripper." Her eyes cloud. "I moved here from Lincolnville. There's a strip club there. Harry's."

I nod. Harry's is kind of notorious.

"It wasn't a good scene. At all," she says quietly. I didn't want to strip anymore, so I came here, but some of the guys found out that's where I used to work, and they were looking to… take advantage." Jewel smiles softly. "Cas was the only one that didn't assume I was public property just because of my past. I think he told the other guys to back off of me, too, because after the first week or so, things settled down." She looks at me now. "I'm no prude, but I like to decide who I sleep with, you know?"

There's a small lump forming in my throat. As hard as my life has been sometimes, I get the feeling that Jewel's has been much harder. "Yeah. I know."

She takes a deep breath and lets it out. "So anyway. Cas is one of the good ones. And he's obviously really into you." She quirks up her lips into a grin. "He's hot, too. Lucky you."

I can't help it. I laugh. "Yeah, he definitely has that going for him."

"So, are you two… you know… Are you *exclusive*?" Jewel's eyes are wide and bright with curiosity.

I shouldn't say any more. But, truth be told, it's kind of a relief to talk it out loud. Like it makes it more real.

"Yes," I admit. "For now, anyway."

"Oh, gosh!" she squeals. "That's so exciting!"

I grin — her enthusiasm is infectious. "We're keeping it a secret for now, though," I tell her.

"Oh, sure, I gathered that," she nods sagely. "Don't worry, honey. Your secret's safe with me." She reaches over and squeezes my hand, and I can't help but feel a wave of affection for this sweet, kind girl, who seems so innocent in spite of everything.

Just then, Noah comes back out with his little backpack and his drawings. I take the backpack and carefully put the papers inside. "How about we take ours home, and let Jewel keep the one of her?" I suggest.

"Okay!" Noah nods. He hands it to Jewel, who kneels down and thanks him with a hug.

"Thanks, kiddo!" she says. "You take care, now, okay? I'll see you next week and you can tell me all about preschool."

I open the door and hold it for Noah to go through. We wave goodbye to Jewel and then walk out to the car. Noah's talking a mile a minute, which means one thing: he's about to crash. Sure enough, I get him strapped into his seat, and by the time we're halfway home, he's already asleep and snoring softly. I smile at my little boy adoringly as I look at him in the rearview mirror. I'm glad Jewel fed him something, because I think he's down for the count.

Which means I can actually have grown-up food for dinner for a change.

I made decent tips today at the clubhouse. Maybe I should splurge on some Chinese delivery, I think jubilantly.

My stomach rumbles in agreement.

Chapter 24

JENNA

I'm contemplating the very serious choice of sesame chicken vs. salt and pepper shrimp as I park my car, hoist a sleeping Noah into my arms, and climb up the stairs to my apartment. I fumble with my keys for a few seconds, then finally unlock my door and push it open.

And somehow, I manage to keep from screaming at the sight of the man sitting at my kitchen table.

"Dad!" I squeak. Taking a deep breath to calm my racing heart, I continue in a loud whisper. "What the hell are you doing here? How did you get in? You scared me half to death!"

"Jenna, I need to talk to you," he says, in a voice I've heard before.

It's the voice he uses when he needs something from me.

"Good God, Dad, you could have just called," I hiss. Then I guiltily remember the four voicemails from him that I still haven't responded to.

"Okay, look," I sigh. "Let me put Noah down. I'll be out in a couple minutes."

Thankfully, Noah's still asleep in my arms, and my near-panic attack didn't wake him. I carry him into his bedroom and lay him down on the bed. Pulling the covers over him, I decide that I'll change him into his jammies later. Then I turn around and prepare to face my father.

When I go back into the main room, he hasn't moved at all. He's still sitting there with his elbows on the table and his chin on his fist, staring into space like a hanged man.

When I come over him, he nods vaguely and tells me to have a seat. I pull out one of the mismatch chairs and sit down facing him. "Why are you here, Dad?" I ask, deciding to get right to the point."

"I need a favor." There's no preamble, none of the chatty questions about how I'm doing that he usually likes to pad a conversation with before jumping into the ask. He's not looking at me, and his eyes look strangely vacant.

Whatever this is, it must be serious. I'm used to Dad playing people's emotions to get what he wants. But that doesn't feel like what this is.

"Do you want something to drink?" I ask, standing up. Suddenly I want a few more seconds before I have to hear what's going on with him.

He tiredly accepts a beer from me, and I pour myself a glass of cheap red wine. When I've served both of us, I sit down again and take a deep breath.

"Okay," I say. "What's going on?"

"I need you to convince your club to do a deal."

Whatever I was expecting, it sure as hell wasn't that.

"What?" I'm dumbfounded. "What deal? Why *me*?"

"Because you have your brother's ear. And Casper's."

Casper's…? None of this makes sense. Sure, Dad knows I tend bar at the clubhouse. But why would he assume that Angel would listen to me about anything having to do with club business? And how would Dad know whether I have Cas's ear specifically?

Before I can ask any of this, though, Dad starts telling me about the deal in question. "Jenna, you know I have a history with the club. That Rock Anthony and I have entered into certain… partnerships… over the years that benefit both the Lords of Carnage and the town of Tanner Springs."

And especially the mayor *of Tanner Springs,* I think to myself sarcastically, but I don't say anything.

"A bit ago, I went to the club asking them for a loan to get me the development deal I've been working on south of town," he continues. For the first time, I notice how ashen my father's face is. "I thought for sure they'd say yes. I was willing to give them a very *advantageous* interest rate on the loan, and a damn good return on their investment. And I know for a fact they can use the money.

"But the deal got voted down." His shoulders sag. "Rumor has it it was a pretty close vote. And that both Angel and Cas voted against me." He looks at me now, his eyes hopeful. "I want you to convince them it's in the best interest in the club to do this deal with me."

Rumor has it... I know he must mean that Rock Anthony told him how the vote went down.

I sit back in my chair, trying to take it all in. My mind is reeling with questions. Why would Angel vote against the deal if our dad wanted it — and if Rock wanted it? And I'm guessing Rock probably does want it, or he wouldn't have told my dad about all this. What's wrong with the deal? Why did Cas vote against it? And how would my dad know whether I "have Cas's ear," as he puts it?

I thought Cas and I had been pretty careful about keeping what was going on with us a secret. We never let ourselves be seen in any sort of compromising position at the club. It's not like we'd been on any "dates" out and about in Tanner Springs. Until right now, the only person I thought knew about us was Jewel. But maybe I was wrong. Still, I knew for sure Dad hadn't seen us together — unless he'd happened to see me on the back of Cas's bike at some point?

Whatever's happening, warning bells are inside my head. I decide to play as dumb as I can.

"Dad," I begin. "Look, I don't know how I could have any influence in this. I mean, I've never talked to Angel about any club stuff. Or Cas." I spread my hands wide. "I wouldn't even know how, to be honest. The Lords keep their business between them."

"You've got to try," he says stubbornly, shaking his head. "I *need* this deal, Jenna."

Exasperation starts to well up inside me. "Well, why is this one deal so important?" I counter. "And if it's such a big deal, why can't you just go to the club and try to convince them yourself?"

"I already have." He pulls himself up straight for a second, but then all the fight seems to leave him, and he slumps, defeated-looking, in his chair. "Jenna Lee. I can't tell you everything. But please." He looks at me with eyes full of desperation. "My life is in your hands."

He never calls me Jenna Lee. Or rather, he never calls me that anymore. It was his nickname for me when I was a little girl — too little to realize that the scraps of affection that he gave me were just that: scraps. These days, he only called me Jenna Lee when he wanted to soften me up.

Still, I can't escape the fact that the look in his eyes is one of sheer terror. It's not a look that he could fake — and I know his acting skills well, having seen him use them on me and others for years.

My father is scared. *Really* scared. And right or wrong, he thinks I'm the only one who can help him.

I feel trapped, but there's no way I can refuse my own father when I see how much this means to him. Sighing, I scoot my chair next to his and give him a brief hug.

"Okay, Dad," I tell him. "I don't know if it will work, but I promise. I'll do my best."

Chapter 25

CAS

The next day is Jenna's day off from work, so I don't see her until early in the evening, once the club business I have to attend to is taken care of. I call her from the road and ask her what she's up to. She tells me to come by for dinner, and I turn the bike around and head off in the direction of her place.

When I get there, I park the bike in one of the spaces reserved for the tattoo parlor. Hannah, one of the tattoo artists who also staffs the front desk, waves at me through the window. I raise a finger to her in greeting. The club knows all the people who work at Rebel Ink, since they're our go-to place to get our ink done. They've probably done hundreds of tattoos for us over the years. Almost every tat I've got is the artwork of one or another of them.

"Hey, handsome." Hannah sticks her head out the door of the shop. She's tall and saucy, with fire-engine red hair and tattoos covering most of her upper body below the neck.

"Hey, gorgeous," I reply easily.

"Been seeing a lot of you around here lately." She nods at the stairwell that leads to Jenna's place. "You got something going on up there?"

I grin at her. "You know I don't kiss and tell." Hannah and I fucked once, about a year and a half ago. It's not common knowledge. She asked me to keep it a secret afterwards because she'd just broken up with Bruno, another tattoo artist at Rebel Ink. Apparently, Bruno was having a little trouble letting go of the relationship. Hannah didn't want him to find out she was banging other people, lest he get jealous and belligerent.

Hannah steps through the doorway to chat. She winks and glances up toward Jenna's apartment. "She's a cutie-pie, that one. I kinda had my eye on her myself, but it looks like you got there first."

I laugh. "I don't think she swings that way, but yeah, I think the ship has sailed on this one."

Hannah raises her eyebrows. "Oh? Is this serious?"

I lower my voice and lean in. "Like I said, I don't kiss and tell," I say, my tone conspiratorial.

"Well, damn, man." She high-fives me. "It couldn't happen to a nicer guy. Good for you, dude." She grins. "Now go get you some!"

I laugh and tell her I'll be coming in for some ink sometime in the next couple of weeks. Hannah heads back into the shop. I'm just about to climb the stairs to Jenna's place when I catch a slight movement out of the corner of my eye.

I turn to see that Charlie Hurt. He's the cheap bastard who owns this place and lives next door. He's sitting in a broken-down lawn chair in his front yard. Charlie's peering at me keenly, and I realize he's been watching my convo with Hannah. When I turn and stare him in the eye, he breaks my gaze and acts like he doesn't notice me.

My fist reflexively clenches. I never liked that creepy fucker.

I shrug it off and head up the stairs to find that the door to Jenna's apartment is open except for the screen. I tap on it and step inside.

Jenna's in the kitchen, and gives me a quick wave while she stirs something. Noah is sitting on the floor next to the couch, a small mound of toys sitting beside him. He looks up at me with a wide, innocent grin.

"Hi, Cas!" he cries. "Wanna play cars?"

"Sure, buddy," I laugh. "Just let me say hi to your mom first."

I walk over to Jenna, who's giving me a smile of her own. My pulse quickens, as it always does when she looks at me.

"Hey, you," she murmurs as I wrap my arms around her.

"Hey, yourself." I kiss her deeply, our tongues dancing, until I feel my dick start to rise to the occasion. I pull away and detach myself from her before it gets too out of hand. "What's for dinner? Smells good."

"Lime chicken," she tells me. "It's something I can get Noah to eat, as long as it's not too 'lime-y.' And I hope you're okay with broccoli. He thinks they look like trees, so he likes them."

"I'll eat whatever you're cooking," I say, reaching down to cup her ass.

"Fresh," she murmurs, pretending to swat me away.

I go back into the living area and plop down on the floor next to Noah. "So, what are we playing?" I ask.

He shrugs. "Just cars." He picks up a small toy motorcycle and holds it out for me to look at. "That's your bike!" he tells me.

"Wow," I nod. "It sure does look like my bike."

"Uncle Angel gave him that," Jenna calls out from the kitchen, a small note of disapproval in her voice.

"Yeah, Uncle Angel says I can ride with him on his motorcycle someday. When I'm bigger."

"Over my dead body," Jenna murmurs.

Noah's peering at me now, a tiny frown on his face. "Uncle Angel says your name is Ghost," he declares.

"It's not my name, exactly. It's my road name," I explain. "Kind of like a nickname."

"Are you a ghost?" he asks me solemnly, his eyes wide.

I grin. "No, I'm not. See?" I hold out my arm and have him feel it. "Solid as a rock. If I was a ghost, you could put your arm right through me."

"Then why do they call you ghost? If you're not a ghost?" he says, confused.

"Well, they call your uncle Angel 'Angel,'" I reason. "Is he an angel?"

In the kitchen, I hear Jenna snort.

"Noooo…" Noah says, frowning as he thinks about this. "He doesn't have wings."

"Exactly," I agree. "Sometimes, people just have silly nicknames. Like how your mom calls you bug. Are you a bug?"

Noah giggles. "No way!"

"Well, there you go," I nod sagely.

"And you call me buddy!" he crows.

"That's because it's a good nickname. And because we're buddies, right?"

"Yup!" he agrees, nodding his head furiously. I hold out my hand and he slaps it energetically. Just then, Jenna comes out with a stack of plates and silverware for the table. Her face has changed, just a hint, but it's there: She looks serious. Something's bothering her.

Wordlessly, I get up and take the plates from her. "You okay?" I ask.

"What? Oh. Yeah. I'm just a little tired is all." Her gaze flickers away from me. I want to ask more, but I don't press it.

Jenna turns and goes back into the kitchen. I put the plates and silverware around, then go grab some milk for Noah and a couple beers for us. A few minutes later, we're seated around the table, talking and eating together. Noah's telling me all about his new preschool, and how excited he is for Monday to come. Jenna's looking at him with such pride, but I can tell without even asking that it's freaking her out a little that her kid is almost old enough for kindergarten.

As I sit there and listen to Noah and watch my beautiful, gorgeous Jenna across the table from me, I think about how anyone who was looking in the window right now would just assume we were a family.

And hell. Maybe we could be.

The thought occurs to me for the first time, and it's like a lightning bolt at first. Why I don't shrug it off immediately, I don't know. But instead, I spend a minute or so just imagining it. Imagining that this is our life, and that I'm Noah's dad. After all, I could adopt him, right?

The idea feels totally different than I would have thought it would. There's a deep tug down in my gut. A deep feeling of longing. Of wanting something more than I've wanted anything in a very long time.

The only other time I can remember is when I started prospecting for the Lords. I wanted to be part of something. A brotherhood.

A family.

Now, I find myself wanting a *real* family. One of my own. With Jenna.

And the scariest thing is?

It doesn't scare me.

After dinner, I help Jenna with the dishes — which still amazes her, even though I've done it before. She hates drying, so I position myself next to her and take the hot plates and silverware from the rinse rack, dry them, and put them away. Noah's had his bath already, so she hustles him off to brush his teeth, and I sit flipping channels on the tube and wait for her to be done.

At bedtime, Noah specifically asks for me to come in and do story time with him. For a second, I have visions of him expecting me to do different goofy voices for all the characters in his book, and almost say no. But as it turns out, Noah likes to read his own bedtime stories. So I sit there on his tiny-ass bed, trying not to fall off, as he reads me a story about a cat named Pete who goes to the beach. As he's following along the text with his finger, sounding out all the words, I glance up to see Jenna standing in the doorway. There's a tiny little smile on her face, and her eyes are soft. I give her a wink and turn back to Noah's book.

When he's finished reading, Jenna comes to tuck him in. I give him a fist bump and tell him goodnight. Then I go back out to the living room so the two of them can finish their nightly ritual. Ten minutes later, she comes out and joins me on the couch.

"I never thought I'd see the day when a big, bad motorcycle rider would be listening to a four-year-old read Pete the Cat," she says, snuggling up to me.

"Look, that book is seriously interesting," I protest. "And when that big wave comes?" I shake my head. "I thought for sure Pete was a goner. Goosebumps."

Jenna starts laughing so hard she snorts, and then she raises her hand to her mouth in embarrassment and starts laughing even harder.

"Oh, my God!" she finally manages to gasp out as tears stream down her cheeks. "I can't believe I just *snorted*!" She erupts into fresh peals and then snorts again. For a second, I'm afraid she's gonna hyperventilate. But it's fucking adorable to see her so helpless with laughter.

I go to the kitchen to grab her a glass of water and give her time to calm herself. When I get back, she's still tittering and wiping at her eyes. "Oh, my God," she giggles as she accepts the glass from me. "I haven't laughed that hard in forever." She takes a long drink and then closes her eyes for a moment, breathing deeply to catch her breath. "I can't believe I didn't wake up Noah."

I pull her into my lap. "I guess I'm just gonna have to figure out a way to keep you quiet somehow." My mouth covers hers and Jenna moans softly, pressing her breasts against my chest.

"Stay the night," she whispers when I break away.

"You sure?" I ask.

"Yes. I'm sure." Her eyes are shining, and there's an undercurrent of lust in her voice.

My cock stands at attention. "I can make sure to be up and out of here before Noah wakes up tomorrow," I rasp.

Jenna bites her lip seductively. "Let's play that by ear for now."

I stand up from the couch and carry Jenna into her bedroom. When I've undressed her and kissed her all over, I pull her onto me and lower her onto my waiting shaft. I watch as she takes her pleasure, riding as quietly as she can, until finally Jenna shatters around me and I lose control, filling her with my explosion and trying not to shout the house down.

Afterwards, we whisper quietly in the dark.

"You know," she tells me, "I always had a crush on you. For years, growing up."

"Seriously?" This is news to me.

She nods. "I was heartbroken that all we had was a fling."

I'm surprised, and maybe even just a little mad. "You're the one who left, Jenna. It wasn't a fling for me. It wouldn't have been one." Even as I say the words, I realize they're true. I remember now how it felt when she left. How pissed I was. I spent the next few weeks getting into fights with anyone I could manage to rile up.

"You shouldn't have let me go." Jenna whispers. "You should have made me stay."

A rumble of laughter rolls through me. "*Made* you stay? Jenna Abbott, I caught on pretty damn quick that no one can tell you what to do." I kiss the top of her head. "Except that little boy of yours. Seems like Noah has you wrapped around his little finger."

Jenna doesn't say anything. She's quiet for long enough that I think she's fallen asleep. When she does start talking again, she changes the subject.

"Can I ask you something?"

"Sure. About what?"

"About the club." Her hand goes to my chest. "How much can women know about club business?"

I think about it. "Old ladies can know a fair amount," I say carefully.

She raises her head to look at me. "Am I your old lady?"

"You want to be?" I ask her. "I sure as shit know I can't make you do anything you don't want to do."

Her eyes shine in the dark. "Yes. I want to be."

"Well, then. There you are." I kiss her deeply. "You taste sweeter as my old lady."

"I wonder if I'll *feel* different as your old lady," she says saucily, wiggling her eyebrows at me. I'm instantly hard.

"Only one way to find out," I say, reaching for her.

Chapter 26

JENNA

"So, can I ask you about the club?" I say as we lie in the dark.

"You're my old lady. You can always ask." Cas pauses. "Old habits die hard, though. I'm not used to telling anyone anything about the Lords. What do you want to know?"

"Just… what's it like, being in an MC?"

"Being in *an* MC, or being in *this* one?"

"This one, I guess."

Part of me expects him to just brush me off, but he doesn't. "Huh. It's… like a family. Although the club doesn't feel much like a family these days," he says darkly.

"How so?" I ask.

He shrugs. "Everything's tense. Seems like everyone's out for themselves instead of a brotherhood like it's supposed to be."

Cas mentions a few names and how some of them are getting pissed about money issues. He talks a little about how the club is starting to have pressure from outside for the first time, with a rival club moving into territory south of town, too close to Tanner Springs for comfort. In a voice tinged with bitterness, he says that Rock doesn't seem to notice, or if he does he doesn't seem to care.

I'm feeling awkward and nervous about bringing up what I have to. But I also recognize that Cas just gave me the best opening I'm likely to get.

"So… the deal you voted on yesterday," I say slowly. "About the loan to my dad for the development. Is that part of the tension?"

Cas sits up and looks at me sharply, his eyes gleaming in the dark. "How do you know about that?"

I freeze for a second, trying to think of a good excuse, but I realize I can't lie to Cas. "My dad came by to talk to me," I admit. "He asked me to try to convince the club to change their minds."

Cas frowns. "It's already been voted on." His expression is frank. "I was one of the ones who voted against it. I'm sorry, Jenna, but it didn't feel right." He sighed. "Angel voted against it too, by the way."

I nod. "I know." *Shit.* I'm feeling like I'm between a rock and a hard place. I don't want to try to push Cas in a direction he doesn't want to go. I don't know the details of this deal, but I trust Cas's judgment. If he feels like there's something off about it, he might be right.

Hell, knowing my father, I wouldn't be surprised.

Still. I told Dad that I'd try to help him.

So I do.

"Was the vote close?" I ask.

Cas lets out a breath. "Yeah."

"Well…" I murmur, hating myself a little, "Can you put it up to a vote again?"

Cas is about to respond when there's a noise at the door. I look over to see that the doorknob is turning. "Holy shit!" I whisper, clutching the sheet to me, but Cas stops me.

"It's okay," he says. "I locked the door."

"Mommy?" Noah's little voice comes from the other side.

"Yes, bug?" I motion for Cas to put something on. He reaches down and grabs his boxer briefs from the pile of clothes on the floor.

"I'm scared!"

"Okay, honey, just a second!" Looking around frantically, I find my panties and put them on, then in desperation pull Cas's T-shirt over my head. It hangs down almost as long as a dress on me.

Cas looks over and gives me a low whistle. "Nice," he says appreciatively.

"Mommy!"

"Coming!" I unlock the door and open it to find Noah clutching Chip-Chip, his eyes wide and frightened.

"I heard noises. I heard people talking."

Oh. We woke him up, I guess. Apparently we weren't whispering as softly as I thought we were.

"It's okay, baby. It was just Cas and me talking."

The words slip out before I really think about what I'm saying. I still hadn't figured out whether I was going to have Cas stay tomorrow to be here when Noah woke up, but I guess that problem's solved now, for better or worse.

But if I thought having to explain to Noah why he stayed was going to be difficult, it turns out I was wrong. Without a word, Noah toddles over to the bed and gets in, curling up to Cas for protection.

I freeze, and wait for Cas's reaction. I'm not sure what I'm expecting, but I watch in amazement as he puts his muscled arm around Noah and settles him in so he can sleep between us.

The two of them look so natural like that that I freeze for a moment, just watching them together. My God, it's so obvious they're father and son to anyone who looks closely. Noah has Cas's eyes, and his dark hair. Even his jawline looks like a miniature version of Cas's square one.

"That's because we're buddies, right?" I can hear Cas saying to Noah earlier tonight. *Buddies.* Suddenly, I want to cry. How will I ever tell Cas Noah's his son? How will I ever manage to explain to him why I didn't tell him right away? *How could I have left it so long?* I think in desperation. Things are going so well between us. Somewhere along the way, I think I've fallen in love with him. Now, I can't see any way to tell him about Noah that won't ruin everything.

I watch as Noah snuggles into the pillow, his thumb sneaking toward his mouth. My God, what will I do — what will *we* do — if I've ruined the possibility of a future with Cas? What if telling Cas that I kept this a secret from him for almost five years makes him so angry that he leaves us?

"Cas!" I blurt out, even though it's impossible, I can't tell him now with Noah here between us. But he puts a finger to his lips.

"Sshhh!" he whispers, motioning for me to come over. "Come on, let's go to sleep."

So, because there's nothing I can do right now, I get into bed and watch as Cas calms Noah until he falls asleep.

When finally Noah's breathing begins to even out, Cas looks up to find me staring at him. "What?" he says.

I'm seconds from telling him. If Noah wasn't between us, I would do it. But I just can't. Not when everything feels so right. I can't bear to wreck everything right now.

Instead, I give him a little smile. "It's just crazy to see you like this. The big bad MC man. I never pictured you as the family type."

He shrugged. "I never had much of a family growing up. My dad and my grandma raised me, but I was kind of an afterthought. A family is something I always wanted. That's why I joined the MC."

I knew his grandmother and his dad growing up, from seeing them around town, but I didn't know much else about Cas's family life. I resist the urge to tell him I'm sorry.

"But brotherhood has nothing on this," he continues with a grin. "C'mon, we should go to sleep. I wore you the hell out already tonight."

"Do you want to move Noah?" I ask him.

"Nah. Let him sleep here. He's not hurting anyone. Though," he smirks, "you could do with a bigger bed."

We pull the covers over us, and I lie in the darkness for close to an hour, my head a swirl of conflicting emotions. I listen to Noah's and Cas's deep, even breathing and tell myself to remember this, to record every second of this, and how it feels. Because I'm afraid it can't last. And even though it will be painful as hell to remember it after it's over, right now it's the most beautiful moment of my life.

Chapter 27

CAS

The next morning, the three of us are eating breakfast — pancakes, because Noah asked for them, and bacon, because *hello, bacon* — when Jenna suddenly says, "Uh-oh."

"What?" I set down my coffee mug and look at her curiously.

"Uh. I just thought of something." She glances at Noah. "Bug, Cas and I are going to go in the bedroom for a couple minutes to talk about something. You holler if you need anything, okay?"

Noah rolls his eyes. "Mom, if it's grown-up stuff, you don't need to leave. It's too boring for me to listen to, anyway."

I laugh. "You got a point, Noah." But I get up and follow Jenna into the bedroom, anyway.

"You sure this isn't just an excuse to get me into bed?" I murmur as I grab her ass.

"Sadly, no," she shakes her head. "I just thought of something kind of... I don't know. Weird."

"What is it?"

She sits down on the bed and I sit with her. "You know when my dad came over a couple days ago to talk to me about the loan deal with the club?"

"Yeah." I still don't know what to do about it like Jenna asked me to, and I'm a little afraid she's going to ask me about it.

"Well," she continues, "The whole conversation with him felt really weird to me at the time. I couldn't figure out why he thought I would have any influence with the club. Why he thought I'd be able to change their minds." She looks at me, her expression strange. "He said, 'You have Angel's ear. And Casper's.' I didn't think about it much at the time, but the more I think about it, the more it bugs me. There's no way he should know I'd have your ear. I'm almost positive he shouldn't know about you and me."

"Huh." I'm quiet for a moment, thinking. "So you think, what? That Angel's figured out about us? You think he told your dad?" I ask.

"I dunno," she frowns. "No, not really. It doesn't make sense. If he does know about us, he sure hasn't said anything to me about it. You'd think he'd have asked one of us to make sure, first."

I turn it over in my head for a few seconds. "Yeah, I don't think it was Angel," I say finally. "Something tells me he won't take it quietly, when he does find out."

"You think he's going to want to fight you?" Jenna looks at me.

"Yeah. But don't worry about it. It'll be fine. He'll land a few punches, and we'll call it a day." I wasn't really sure it'd be dealt with that easily, but no reason to alarm Jenna about that now.

"So, if it's not Angel — and like I said, I don't think it is — what do you think is going on?" I ask.

"I'm not sure," she says slowly. "Maybe Dad's having me watched, or something?"

"That's fucked up," I say angrily. "Who would have someone spying on their own kid?"

"Yeah, I know. It does sound crazy, but I can't think of anything else." She shakes her head. "The thing is, I get the feeling my dad's involved in something. Maybe something bad." She meets my gaze. "He seemed really desperate for this loan with the Lords to go through when I talked to him. I get the feeling that whatever he's involved in, maybe he's not the one in control. He seemed so worn out and stressed when I saw him." She pauses, and then frowns, almost like she's disagreeing with herself. "Cas, do you think it's possible he's being blackmailed?"

I open my mouth to reassure her, but then something clicks in my head.

The Abe Abbott I know is a wheelin', dealin' son of a bitch. I'd never say that to Jenna about her own father, but it's true.

The shit he's been involved in, she doesn't know the half of. And I'm not about to tell her any of it.

But if there's one thing I do know about him, it's that he's not above breaking the law to get what he wants. And he's sure as hell not above playing people off each other to get what he wants.

Including his own daughter, I'd bet.

He's no stranger to corruption. And if *he's* scared of something? That's not a good fucking sign. If he's scared, then he has good reason to be. I'd guarantee it.

"Cas?" Jenna interrupts my thoughts. "What are you thinking?"

"I have to go out for a little bit." I tell her, rising. "Call Jewel and get her to take Noah if you can. I'll be back in a couple of hours."

* * *

I come back to Jenna's place to find her alone.

"I brought you a present," I tell her when she lets me in.

"A present?" Jenna's confused. "What, you ran out to get me flowers or something?"

"Hardly," I say grimly.

I reach back and pull the gun out of the waistband of my jeans. Jenna lets out a little shriek when she sees it.

"Jesus, Cas…" she breathes.

"It's for you to protect yourself." My eyes lock on hers. "And to protect Noah."

"Do you really think that's necessary?"

I take a deep breath and let it out. "I think it's better to consider the possibility."

Jenna is frightened, but she doesn't argue.

"Do you know how to shoot?" I ask her.

"No," she answers in a small voice.

I nod. "I thought maybe you didn't. Come on," I say, pushing open her door. "We're going to the range."

The gun is a Smith and Wesson Shield, nine millimeter. It's a big enough pistol to stop someone in his tracks, but still small enough and easy enough to handle that it should be less intimidating for someone like Jenna, who's small and who's never shot a gun before.

Once we're at the range, I grab us some targets and some eye and ear protection. I explain some of the basics, show her the magazine and how to load ammo into it, and talk to her about recoil. I let her ask as many questions as she wants and give her some time to handle the gun while it's unloaded, so she can start to feel more comfortable with it.

I can tell she's a little scared at first, and that's as it should be. It always worries me when some jackass picks up a gun for the first time and acts like it's a goddamn water pistol. When it's time for her to shoot, she takes it seriously and gives it all her concentration. I see right away that she's got a good eye. She's a quick study, and after helping her figure out the sights, she's shooting consistently within a few inches of the bullseye after an hour.

We quit when I can see she's starting to get tired. I'm feeling a little better knowing that she's at least capable of handling the gun. Jenna seems to look a little less worried, too. She even asks me if we can come back to the range again soon, to practice.

"Of course, darlin'," I tell her, pulling her in for a kiss. "You're a natural, do you know that?"

"Oh, I don't know about that," she smiles, but I can tell she's proud of herself. And she should be.

We walk out of the range, and when we get to my bike, Jenna puts a hand on my arm. "Thanks for doing this for me, Cas. But the more I think about it, the more I think we're probably overreacting about Dad." She shakes her head. "We must have just slipped up and he saw us together. Or maybe one of his friends saw us and said something. Dad's got a lot of friends in this town. It's probably nothing."

"You may be right," I nod. "But just in case, I want you to keep the gun handy. I'll come back home with you and figure out a safe place to store it so you can get to it quickly, but it's still away from Noah."

"Okay. And Cas?"

"Yeah?"

"Please do what you can for my dad." Her voice is sad. "That's all I'll ask."

I cup her chin and raise her face to mine. "I promise, babe. I'll do whatever I can."

Chapter 28

JENNA

Riding back to my place with Cas, I'm still feeling the adrenaline rush from spending an hour at the gun range. I've always been terrified of guns, truth be told. But even so, I can't help but admit to myself how powerful it felt to shoot such a precision machine. Every time I hit the target close to the bullseye, I felt like cheering. I felt like a badass. Even though afterwards, I kept remembering why I was learning to do this, and suddenly wanted to throw up.

The vibrations from the bike calm me down a little, and I snuggle in tighter to Cas. Even though there's a slight possibility I might be in danger, he makes me feel safe. The solid heat of him makes me feel protected. Calm.

When we get back to my apartment, Cas looks around until he finds a little cubby high up in my bedroom closet. He shows me how to store the gun there safely, so that I can reach it on a moment's notice. It's a good spot, far too high for Noah to get up to, even if he found the highest chair in our apartment.

I'm scared to have a gun in the house, in a way. It's not something I ever considered doing before. But given that we don't really know what's going on right now, I'm also a little scared *not* to.

"That should about do it," Cas eventually says, closing my closet door. "You did good today, girlie."

"Girlie?" I snort. "Seriously?"

"Hey, nothing wrong with being a girl," he says, drawing me to him. "Girls can kick ass. You just proved that out on the range."

"Yeah, well, let's hope I never have to prove that." My heart starts to pound again with nervousness at the thought. But then Cas bends down and kisses me, and the pounding changes to a fluttering. "Cas," I breathe as he presses me to him. "We still have a little while before I have to go pick up Noah."

His lips graze against my neck. "I like the way you think, girlie."

I'm about to protest again, but before I can his hand comes to my breast, his thumb sliding against the hardening nub of my nipple. "Oh!" I gasp, my hips bucking forward on their own power.

My heartbeat races beneath his lips, and before I know it I'm trembling with desire. My head falls back as he pulls open my shirt, then tugs down on the bra cups. A low moan comes from deep in his throat as his lips close over one taut bud. The vibrations from his voice tease me even before his tongue begins to flick and caress my desperate flesh.

Straining and mewling with pleasure, my fingers thread through his hair as he laps and suckles me. Between my legs, a low, almost painful ache has already started. I could never have believed it, but every time with Cas just gets better. The more our bodies know each other, the more I need what I know only he can give me. It feels almost like we were meant to be together. I've never believed in anything so cheesy, but the way our bodies respond to each other -- the way he seems to know exactly what to do to make me scream in pleasure -- it feels almost like this is what the two of us were made for. Each other.

As Cas flicks his tongue against my nipple, one hand slides down my skin, painfully slowly. Eventually, his fingers dip down inside my shorts. At first, they drift over my panties, just the lightest touch, and I strain toward him, desperate for more. Finally, he moves the thin fabric aside to find my wet, throbbing center. I gasp as his fingers find my slickness. Shivering, I wait in anticipation as he groans and reaches to unbutton my shorts and push them down.

Cas's head comes up to kiss me again, drawing my bottom lip between his teeth to tug at it just a little. It makes me *wild* with need.

"Do you want this?" he whispers.

"Oh, God, yes…" I breathe. I open my eyes, lids heavy, to stare at him. His expression is hungry.

His fingers continue to slide against my slickness, slowly, so slowly. I move against them, shuddering as he brushes against my taut bud. He traces soft, maddening circles around it, pulling back as I push forward, chuckling deep in his throat. I know he won't give me relief, not yet, and I try to keep my breathing even and hold on until he lets me have what I need. But I know what might make him change his mind.

I reach down and push my hand inside his jeans, finding the hard, hot steel inside. It pulses and throbs at my touch, and I'm rewarded with a deep groan from Cas. "Jesus fuck, it feels good when you do that," he rasps. I continue to stroke, loving the feel of him. I can tell he's working hard to restrain himself, and I'm doing my best to work him up enough that he can't. Suddenly, he hisses my name. "Jenna. I can't wait. I need to have you now."

He slides my shirt and bra off me, then pulls me toward my kitchen table. I'm panting slightly with need as I watch him pull of his shirt and kick off his jeans. His pulsing shaft springs free, and my pussy clenches with want.

"Lie down," he orders me, glancing at the table.

"You sure this thing will hold us?" I gasp.

"I'll buy you another one," he growls. He's not taking no for an answer. With a thrill of excitement, I lie back on the table, putting my feet up where he shows me. A tiny part of me is embarrassed at being this exposed to him, but I'm too turned on to care. He looks down and swears. "Jesus, you are so fucking sexy. My Jenna. My fucking gorgeous Jenna." He slides two thick fingers inside me, and I clamp down on him, my body acting on its own. He starts to stroke me inside, finds this spot he's found before that I didn't even know was there, and oh my God, all of a sudden I'm *so close*, and then everything happens at once as I start to shudder and quake...

"Come for me, Jenna," he urges, and I spasm and clamp around his fingers as I explode into a million pieces. Then his fingers are gone and his mouth is licking and laving at my clit, and I scream his name as I come hard a second time.

I'm still shuddering as he enters me, his cock sliding deliciously against my swollen lips. It's too much, I'm too sensitive, but even so I can't help but want more. "Oh, God, yes, Cas," I moan. "Yes, yes, come inside me."

He slams into me, hard, and I hear him swear before pulling out and slamming into me again, raw and unrestrained. "Fuck, Jenna, I can't fucking get enough of you," he rasps. "I'm gonna fill you up, baby." His muscled thighs flex as he begins to speed up, owning me as I start to spiral upward yet again. He plunges a final time, deeper than ever before, and as he groans and begins to shoot, a third climax rips through me, shaking me to my core.

Then Cas is lifting me up, with him still inside me, and carrying me to the couch. We stay like that, joined together, me wrapped around him and his arms engulfing me. He continues to devour my mouth as we pant and gasp for breath, our hearts racing next to each other.

"Holy fuck," he breathes.

"I'm pretty sure they heard that downstairs," I say, having recovered just enough to be embarrassed at the thought.

Laughter rumbles from his throat. "Let them hear. Gives them something to aspire to."

He kisses me again, deeply, and then pulls away to look at me. "You're one hell of a woman, you know that, Jenna Abbott?"

"That so?" I ask happily.

"Yeah, that's so. Thank Christ you're my old lady. Otherwise I'd have to fight someone for you."

"Old lady," I sigh. "Funny how that sounds so nice when you say it. Never thought I'd be happy for someone to call me old."

He grins and dips his head down to nip at my neck. "You're not fuckin' old, baby. Shit, even when you *are* old, you won't be old. You'll still be the sexiest fucking thing on wheels."

"You're just saying that to get tail," I smirk.

"No, I'm not," Cas says, his face turning serious. "You are gonna be the hottest old lady any man has ever seen." His thumb comes up to graze my lower lip. "And I plan to be around to see it."

His eyes bore into mine. I try to think of something jokey to say, but the air between us has shifted. "You mean, even when I've got wrinkles and cellulite?" I manage to stammer.

"And gray hair and crow's feet. The whole nine yards." His lips brush mine. "I love you, Jenna Abbott. I told you you were mine. That means for keeps."

It's like the oxygen's been sucked out of my lungs. I can't breathe for a second. Cas Watkins — the boy I've been crazy about for years and years — just told me he loved me.

"Cas," I whisper, fighting back a sudden lump in my throat. "I love you, too."

"I think I knew that," he says with a devilish grin. "But it's nice to know for sure."

I laugh, happy tears springing to my eyes, and fling my arms around him. We kiss, with an intimacy I've never felt before. *This is us*, I think dizzily. *He loves me. We're together.*

He pulls away from me then, with an amused smile. "Sorry to wreck the moment, but we're about five seconds away from leaving a giant wet stain on your couch."

"Oh, shit!" I say, scooting to my feet.

Cas grabs the boxer briefs that are lying in a pile next to the couch and hands them to me. "Here, use these."

"That was the shortest romantic moment I've ever had," I complain, taking them from him to wipe myself.

"I promise to make it up to you," he says with a twinkle in his eye.

As we get dressed, Cas tells me he's got some business to attend to at the club. "I'm sorry to have to leave you, babe. But I promise I'll be back tonight," he says.

"I hope so," I sigh. I tug at the leather cut he's just shrugged back on. I miss him already.

"Just as soon as I can get away," he promises me. "And while I'm there," he continues with a slight frown, "I figure maybe it's about time to tell Angel about us. May as well get it over with."

"Okay," I nod slowly. He's got a point. There's really no point in keeping this a secret any longer.

The time for secrets is over.

It's time to stop pretending, Jenna. A shadow crosses my face as I realize it's time for me to come clean with Cas, as well. *I need to tell him about Noah. Tonight.*

Cas sees me frown and mistakes the reason for it. "It'll be okay," he murmurs, reaching up to caress my cheek. "I promise. Whatever happens won't change anything between you and me."

I hope you're right, I think, suddenly feeling a little sick.

As I walk out with Cas, I notice that Charlie Hurt is outside in his driveway, hammering at something. When he sees us, he stops hammering and glances our way, watching to see what we do. A shudder of disgust runs through me, and I resist the urge to stick my tongue out at him. I do stop and stare pointedly at him, though, and he quickly looks away and starts hammering again.

Cas gets on his bike, and I get in my car to go pick up Noah. As I watch him drive away in my rearview mirror, I have a moment of panic when I realize that tonight might be the end of everything. A wave of nausea and dizziness comes over me, and I have to sit in the car for a moment and breathe deeply. My stomach has been bothering me for a couple of days now. I chalk it up to anxiety, what with everything going on right now. I'm scared that something's going on with my father that he's not telling me. I'm nervous about Angel's reaction when Cas tells him about us. But most of all, I'm scared that when I tell Cas he's Noah's father, he'll hate me, and everything between us will crumble like a house with no foundation.

It has to be okay, I tell myself as I put a hand to my racing heart. *It has to. If Cas loves me, he'll forgive me.*

Won't he?

Putting the car in gear, I drive over to Jewel's place, hoping all the way there that a mistake I made five years ago isn't about to ruin the best thing that's ever happened to me.

Chapter 29

CAS

As soon as I pull up to the club, the front door comes crashing open on its hinges. I look over in surprise to see Angel burst through the doorway. He comes stalking toward me, a murderous look in his eye that I've only seen a couple of times before.

"Oh, shit," I mutter. This can only be one thing.

When Angel's about halfway to me, he starts to yell and wave his arms in the air. "You fucking piece of shit! You *fucking* piece of shit!"

He's way too wound up and angry to listen to anything I have to say right now. So I know what I have to do. I swing my leg over the bike and stand to face him, bracing for the inevitable.

"You're fucking my sister?" Angel yells, the veins bulging in his neck. "You goddamn traitor! I'll fucking kill you!"

His fist comes flying toward the left side of my face, and I don't move to block it. Instead, I take the hit, staggering back as he connects hard with my left cheek, right under the eye. *Fuck.* A lightning bolt of pain flashes through my head.

That one, he gets a free pass on, because I deserved it. I'm not taking more than one hit without a fight, though.

I get my feet underneath me, and then brace myself for the second one. He roars and flies at me again, but this time I feint and dodge him, grabbing his arms and pulling him to the ground with me. We scuffle as he struggles to get free and swears a blue streak at me. I manage to keep him from landing another punch, and eventually, when I sense he's starting to tire out, I let him go and stagger back into a crouch. I watch as he scrambles up, waiting to see if he's gonna charge me again.

When he sees that I'm ready for him now, and that I mean business, he squints angrily at me but doesn't make a move.

"How did you know?" I rasp, breathing heavily.

"Abe fucking told me," Angel says. He's still seething. "How the fuck does my fucking father know this before I do?" He spits on the ground. "Jesus, when you said no one would touch her, you didn't mean you, huh?"

"Dammit, Angel," I swear. "I know you aren't gonna believe this, but I was coming here to tell you about Jenna and me." Angel snorts, shaking his head in disbelief. "It's true," I persist. "Look, you can ask Jenna about that."

"Why the fuck would I believe Jenna? She goddamn lied to me, too. Both of you can go to hell," he sneers in disgust.

"I'm not lying, Angel. We've been trying to think of how to tell you for a while, now." I take a breath and let it out, then continue more slowly. "It's not something we planned. But this isn't just a meaningless fuck, brother. This is the real deal. Jenna's my old lady now."

Angel's face changes when I say these words. It's maybe the only thing I could have said that would calm him down.

"I mean it when I said I was coming here to tell you, brother," I continue. "You don't have to believe it. But it's true. I'm sorry we kept it from you for so long."

The smallest hint of a smile tugs at one corner of his mouth. "You're serious? Jenna's your old lady?"

I chuckle softly. "Yeah. Never saw it coming, but there it is."

"Shit, man." He stands motionless for a moment. "That's… That's pretty cool, actually." He shakes his head and snickers. "Except now I gotta know that you two fuck."

I throw my head back and laugh. "Sorry. Kinda comes with the territory."

"Huh. I guess that means we're brothers in more ways than one, then." He grabs my hand and claps me on the back.

"Guess so." I grin, then wince a little at the pain.

"Oh, fuck. Shit, sorry about that, man." Angel's brow creases. "You shoulda told me yourself. If I'd known…"

"Nah, it's okay," I said. "You probably would have punched me anyway. I was ready for it."

He snorts. "Yeah, you might be right. Look, let's go get something cold for your eye. It's already starting to swell up."

I take a step forward as he turns toward the clubhouse. "As long as that something cold comes in a bottle…" I start to say, and then freeze in my tracks.

Something's not right.

Now I know for sure that Angel didn't know about Jenna and me before today.

Angel didn't tell Abe.

Abe told Angel.

Bells are going off in my head, and it's not because Angel just punched me.

Abe's known all along.

"I'll take a rain check, brother," I mutter hastily to Angel. "I've got somewhere I need to be."

I race back toward the bike and fly out of the parking lot like I'm on fire.

I have to get to Jenna.

Chapter 30
JENNA

Cas is pounding on the door like a madman when I open it.

"Sshhh! What is wrong with you?" I whisper crossly. "Noah's sleeping. You're going to wake him up!" My eyes go to his face, which is bruised under his eye and rapidly swelling. "Oh my God, what happened? Did Angel —"

Cas brushes me off with a short wave of his hand. It's obvious he's not really listening to me. He looks like a man possessed as he pushes past me and starts to stalk around the room, his eyes dark and stormy. His boots clomp loudly on the wood floor, and I shush him again, but he doesn't pay any attention. Suddenly, he stops, and stares fixedly for a moment at a spot in the corner.

I'm seriously alarmed now. I've never seen him like this. "Cas!" I cry, forgetting about Noah. "What the hell is —"

"Sshhh!" he hisses, and grabs me by the arm. He leads me out the front door onto the landing, glancing over toward the house next door as he does so.

"We don't need to be *this* quiet," I say, folding my arms. "We just need to —"

"I'm not worried about Noah," he says, cutting me off.

"Cas, what is going on? You're acting like a crazy person."

"Who got you this place?" he demands.

"My dad," I reply, not understanding. "I've told you that before. Why?"

"Has anyone else been in the apartment besides you and Noah since you moved in?"

"You mean besides you?" Frowning, I think back over the weeks. "Well, yeah," I say after a moment. "My dad was here the other night. And, oh, the landlord, of course. The man who lives next door. Charlie." I suppress a shiver. "He came over about a week and a half ago. Said he needed to find the source of a leak or something. I guess water was coming through the ceiling to the tattoo place downstairs."

"Were you in here with him the whole time when he was in the apartment?" Cas is eyeing me intently.

"No," I reply. "Gross. That guy creeps me out. And besides, I had to go to work. So I let him in and then left with Noah."

Cas swears softly and looks back inside with a worried expression.

"Cas, what is it?" I repeat. "Did you find something out?"

"Nothing specific," he mutters. "Just a hunch." He stops to think for a moment. "Do you have a screwdriver? Flathead."

"I think so," I say uncertainly. "Will a Swiss Army knife attachment do?"

"Yeah. That's fine. Okay, let's go back inside. But don't talk."

Don't talk?

I follow him back into the apartment, and go rummage in a kitchen junk drawer. Eventually I find the knockoff Swiss Army knife. I pull out the screwdriver blade and go back into the living room, where Cas is moving around the room, running his hands around the moldings and peering behind shelves.

I hold out the knife and hand it to him. "This is the best I can do," I whisper.

Cal puts his finger to his lips wordlessly. He nods and takes the knife from me, then bends down. I watch him as he starts to unscrew the strike plates to the electrical outlets. On the third one, he lets out a huff of breath and stands up. He holds his hand out to me, and I see that in his palm is a small object. It's about an inch and a half by an inch and a half, and black. It sort of looks like a square domino with no dots on it.

"What is it?" I mouth.

Cas crooks a finger and I follow him back out onto the landing. He tosses the object down on the ground and brings his heel down on it, smashing it.

"It's a bug," he says, turning it over in his palm.

"What?" I cry. "Like, a spy bug?"

"Sshhh," he says urgently, and glances over his shoulder. "There might be more inside."

"Cas, what is going on?" I say urgently, trying to keep my voice low. "You have *got* to explain all this to me, right now!" My heart is starting to race. *I'm being bugged? Does that mean someone's been hearing everything I do?*

"I will," he promises, grabbing my hands in his. "But first, let's go back in and keep looking. I'm going to bet there are a few more of these around somewhere. Once we're pretty sure we've got them all, I'll tell you everything I know."

Cas finally seems to really look at me then, for the first time since he got here. He must see that I'm starting to panic, because his eyes soften and he reaches up to softly caress my face. "Jen. It's okay," he murmurs. "I'm with you. We just need to deal with this right now."

"I know," I say. My voice is starting to shake and I can't seem to control it. I already wasn't feeling very well earlier, and now I'm starting to feel a little wobbly. "I know. I'm just… this is a lot to take in. I just feel kind of… sick, and violated, you know?"

"I know, babe." Tenderly, more tender than I've ever known him to be, he plants a soft kiss on my forehead. "We'll figure this out. I'll get to the bottom of this." His eyes flash with anger. "And I swear to you, whoever's behind all of this is going to pay."

"Yeah," I say miserably. "But what if the person behind it is my father?"

Chapter 31

CAS

Jenna and I do a full sweep of the apartment. We check smoke detectors, wall and ceiling light fittings, lamps, and any other nook and cranny we can think of. We check all the baseboards and moldings. I look around the entire apartment, including Noah's bedroom, for paint discolorations on the walls and ceilings, just in case someone's planted a microcamera in here. We even turn all the furniture upside down and look for holes in the upholstery. It takes over an hour, and at the end of our search we've found three more bugs. I take them outside with me, one by one, and give them the same treatment I gave the first one. As I'm smashing the last one, Jenna comes out to join me.

"Do you really think it was my father?" Jenna asks miserably.

I feel like hell for her, but I can't see anyone else it would be.

"I think it has to be, babe." I run a hand through my hair and take a deep breath. "You know how I went to the clubhouse to tell Angel about us?"

She nods. "I assume that's what this shiner is about," she says, looking at my cheek.

I shrug. "Yeah. No worries about that, though. He punched me, I told him it wasn't just a roll in the hay — that you're my old lady now — and he's cool with it."

"Seriously?" In spite of how scared she is, she giggles. "Men are so weird."

"But that's not the important part right now," I continue. "Here's the thing: I never even got the chance to tell Angel we were together. He already knew." My eyes lock on hers. "Your dad told him."

She frowns in confusion for a second, and then it hits her. "The bugs! Oh my God, you think he knew from the bugs!"

"I do." I wait as she processes this, her face changing from astonishment to dismay to horror. "Oh my God! Do you think he heard us having... *sex*?" She says this last word in a horrified whisper. I almost laugh, but I know she's not in the mood to joke about this.

"Probably not him," I reassure her. "These listening devices are pretty cheap, low-tech versions. The kind you can pick up for less than twenty bucks. I'd be surprised if they had a range of more than half a mile." I raise my chin toward the house next door, and wait for Jenna's eyes to follow mine. "My bet would be him."

Jenna's eyes widen. "Charlie?" Her face contorts in revulsion.

"Yeah," I say in disgust. "It stands to reason that he could be on your dad's payroll. I know from talking to some of the guys downstairs at Rebel Ink that there are some pretty serious code violations down there. But somehow, the city always seems to look the other way. My guess is that Charlie Hurt and your dad have a mutually advantageous arrangement."

Jenna is nodding her head. "I could see that. Charlie is definitely a slumlord." She glances back toward her apartment. "It was kind of hard for me to believe this place was up to code when I moved in." She snorts. "Maybe it's not."

"I've been noticing for a while now that Charlie seems to be outside a lot when we get here, and goes inside his house when we go inside your apartment. I thought it was just a coincidence at first, but…" I shake my head. "I should have figured this out before now."

"Oh, my God…" Jenna breathes. "I don't know how, but that's almost *worse*!" In a disgusted voice, she tells me about how Charlie came over once when she hadn't found a job yet, and suggested an *alternative* way for her to pay rent. "God, the idea that he might be listening in on us and *getting off* on it..." She sticks out her tongue like she's gagging.

A wave of pure, unadulterated fury washes over me, so strong that I have to stop myself from going over there right now and beating that fucker senseless. The only thing that keeps me from doing it is that I want to know the full extent of how much he deserves this beatdown before I give it to him.

"If that piece of *shit* ever touches you or talks to you that way again, you tell me right away, you hear me?" I say, gritting my teeth so hard I think they might break. My hands have curled into fists of their own accord, and god *damn* do I want to punch something right now.

"I promise," Jenna breathes, her eyes wide. She shrinks back just a little bit in fear, and I force myself to pull back and get a grip.

"I'm sorry, babe." *Focus, Cas.* I take a deep breath and make myself let it out slowly, to calm myself down. "Okay. So, let's think about this for a second. I'm gonna assume that your dad isn't just spying on you because he's a possessive father. He must need information for some reason. What info is he looking for?"

"I don't know. I can't think of anything." She looks at me. "And I guess we don't really know whether Charlie came in that day to install the bugs. Maybe they've been here all along, since I moved in." She frowns. "My dad was really pushing for me to move into his house when I told him I was coming to Tanner Springs. I wonder whether there was some reason for that, other than him just wanting to keep an eye on me?"

"Honestly, I doubt it," I say. "If I had to guess, I'd say these bugs are relatively recent. Maybe Charlie started to notice me coming and going over here, and ran over to your dad with the info like a dog with his master's slippers." I run a hand through my hair. "Maybe it just started as a way for your dad to try to gather intel. Maybe that's all there was to it."

Jenna stands up to her full height and seems to pull herself together. "I suppose we can't know the reasons, or when he put them in. What's more important now is, what does he know, assuming it is my dad?"

"At this point, I can't think of who else it could be." I pause for a second, trying to think of any other ways someone might be spying on her. "Have you left your cell phone in the room when your dad was here? He might have installed an audio recorder in it with a SIM card."

"No." She shakes her head. "I'm sure of that. I always keep my phone on me. Besides, my dad barely understands how to operate his own phone. I'm positive he wouldn't have any idea how to do that. Even if someone tried to explain it to him." She cocks her head, then, and looks at me. "But… wait a minute."

"What?" I ask.

"There's actually a functioning land line here," She says. She leads me back inside, over to the divider between the living room and the kitchen. She reaches into a little shelf under the counter and pulls out an old, yellow rotary phone. "I can't believe I just ignored this thing the first time around," she says.

"Holy hell, look at that thing," I say, snorting. "It looks like it's from about nineteen-ninety."

"It could be," she muses. "I couldn't believe it was connected when I moved in."

I pick up the receiver to the corded phone. The tinny dial tone is just audible in the otherwise silent room. I set the handset back into its cradle.

"Have you used it?"

"Not for anything important. I think I made a couple of local calls on it for the novelty, but just for things like ordering pizza." She wrinkles her nose. "The connection's not very good. The line pops a lot when you use it."

I pick it up again and unscrew the mouthpiece. Yup. There's one in here, too. I pull it out silently and show it to her, then set it down on the counter and smash it with the back of the handset.

"Well," Jenna jokes nervously. "I guess they know my favorite pizza is pepperoni and extra cheese."

Down the hall, a small voice yells, "Mommy!"

"Shit," I groan. "I woke up Noah."

"It's okay," Jenna murmurs. "That's the least of our worries." Raising her voice, she calls, "I'm coming, bug!"

"Jenna," I say urgently. "I need to go take care of some stuff. I'll be back later. But in the meantime, you need to hide the gun someplace else. You can't take the chance that Charlie heard us when we hid it."

Her eyes are wide and serious. "Okay. I'll be waiting," she says in a strong voice. A wave of love washes over me to see her so steely and determined.

"You're fucking amazing, you know that?" I bend down and kiss her.

She waves me off. "Call me."

"Will do. Just as soon as I can."

I tell Jenna to lock the door behind me. I need to get to the clubhouse. But first things first.

I take the old wooden stairs two at a time, and cross the yard over to Charlie Hurt's house. Not bothering to knock, I slam open his front door and find that miserable fuck getting out of an old, stained recliner in front of a big boxy TV. His eyes are wide with fear. He makes a break for the back door but I've got his fat ass by the collar before he can get two feet.

Hauling him backwards, I throw him into the chair and pull back one clenched fist. "Who the fuck are you working for?" I say in a low, seething voice. "You've got once chance to answer."

He still looks terrified, but he shakes his head and lets out a high-pitched, nervous laugh. I snort and clock the fucker across the face, hearing the snap as his nose breaks.

"Fuck!" he cries, raising his hands to his face as blood begins to spurt from his nostrils. "Fuck!"

"I told you, you had one chance," I spit. "Let's see if you're a quick learner. Who are you working for?"

He's moaning in pain, rocking back and forth, but he shakes his head again. "I can't," he gurgles.

I punch him again, this time hard in the gut. I watch, impassively, as he leans over and retches. Blood mixed with spit and snot pours from his face.

"I'm pretty sure you can," I tell him. "You want some more, or are you going to tell me what I want to know?"

"I fucking can't!" he half-blubbers, half-cries. "It's worth more than my life."

"Oh, for fuck's sake," I spit out. "You can't tell me Abe Abbott's gonna kill you for telling me you're working for him."

Despite the fact that he's sobbing, Charlie starts to *laugh*. He sounds half-crazy, laugh-crying and holding his leaking face.

"You think it's *Abe* I'm scared of?" he chokes out. "It's not Abe, man." He shakes his head violently back and forth. "There's nothing you can do to me that's as bad as what they'll do if I tell you. Nothing."

This isn't what I'm expecting. This fucker's got "I'm a piece of shit coward" written all over him. It shouldn't have even taken me punching him to get him to spill. Hell, all it should have taken was me *threatening* to punch him.

He's not talking. And he's not lying, either.

Whoever he's working for, this is a hell of a lot bigger than just Abe Fucking Abbott.

I look down in disgust at the filthy fucker. Kneeling down, I get up in his face and grab him by the throat.

"We found your bugs," I tell him, keeping my voice low. He gasps as I begin to constrict his windpipe, clutching at my arm desperately. "I know you've been spying on Jenna. And I swear to God, if you ever come anywhere near her again — if you so much as *look* at her — I will fucking kill you." With my other hand, I pull his head up by the hair until he's looking at me. "You got that? I will fucking shoot you in the head."

He makes a strangled sound that I decide to take for a yes. I tighten my grip around his throat just a little more, for emphasis. When I let go, he lets out a loud sob and buries his head in his hands. I look down to see he's wet himself.

"Time to get that chair cleaned, I guess," I snarl, and turn around to stomp out the way I came. The sounds of Charlie's crying follow me out as the screen door slams behind me.

I immediately head over to my bike and hop on. I need to talk to Angel. Now.

I fire up the engine and kick it into gear, throttling up so fast my tires squeal and skid out from under me for a second. As I head out onto the road, I'm going easily twenty over the speed limit. I'm sure to make it to the clubhouse in less than five minutes, but then I feel the vibration of my phone in my back pocket. Swearing, I slow down a bit and take it out to look.

It's a text from Angel. With an address, and the code we use for "urgent."

"Fuck!" I shout. I throttle down, spin the bike around, and take off as fast as I can in the other direction.

Chapter 32

JENNA

After Cas leaves, I lock the door like he tells me to.

"Mommy," Noah says in a sleepy voice, holding his arms out to me. I slide onto the bed and wrap him in a hug. I take a moment to just breathe him in, love washing over me as I hold my little boy. *I'll keep you safe,* I tell him silently in my head. *I promise that no matter what, I'll keep you safe.*

"I got scared of a loud noise," he murmurs into my chest.

"It's okay, sweetheart," I tell him. "It was just Cas. He had to, uh, fix something, but it made a loud noise."

Noah sits up and looks toward the bedroom door. "Is Cas here?"

"No, bug. He had to go somewhere."

"Oh." His tone is disappointed. Noah looks up at me. "I like it when Cas is here," he says.

My heart constricts. "I do too, honey."

"Is Cas gonna be my daddy?"

I freeze. Somehow, Noah has asked the one question that I have no idea how to answer. All my fears, all my hopes, all my regrets about the past are encapsulated in it.

I sit there paralyzed, unable to answer, and Noah asks me again.

Oh, God.

"I don't know, baby," I finally whisper.

"I want Cas to be my daddy," he declares. "Can we ask him later?"

"I'll tell you what, Noah," I say in a strangled voice. "Let's not ask him just now. Okay?"

Noah frowns, but thankfully he doesn't argue. "Okay. But can we ask him later?"

"We'll see, bug." I kiss him on the forehead and try to blink back tears. "We'll see."

Noah's wide awake now, and I don't have the heart to tell him to just go back to sleep. Since I'm too antsy to sit and read with him, I settle him in with my computer and Chip-Chip and let him watch videos for a while. Then I go back out to the living room to pace and think.

The nausea I've been fighting off and on for the past week is back, and I bow my head and close my eyes as a wave of it washes over me. With everything that's happened today, I'd tried to push it to the back of my mind. But now that Cas is gone, and after Noah's too-astute question, it's harder to ignore. When the wave has passed, I stand up straight and open my eyes.

It's time to find out the answer to something I've been almost too afraid to contemplate.

I remember the first time I used one of these pregnancy tests. At the time, the humiliation of buying the thing was almost more traumatizing than actually taking the test itself. I put it off for weeks, and worked myself into such a frenzy of worry that by the time I actually saw the twin pink lines in the little window, it was almost a relief just to have it over with. Just to have an answer.

This time I'm older, so buying the test was less embarrassing. Even so, I made sure ahead of time that the cashier at the drug store in Tanner Springs wasn't someone I knew before I checked out. Now, as I lock myself in the bathroom and pee on the strip, I'm hit with a sense of déjà vu. Twice in my life, I've been worried I was pregnant. And both times, it was from being with the same guy.

I stare at a tiny hole in the shower curtain, my hands clasped tightly in my lap, and count three and a half minutes in my head, just to be safe. Then I take a deep breath and look at the little stick.

And, both times, the answer was 'yes.'

* * *

I spend the next half-hour wandering around the apartment in a daze. How could this have happened? I've been on the pill for the last two years. Wishful thinking, since I hadn't had sex in much longer than that before I came back to Tanner Springs and started up again with Cas. I guess it's true what they say about the pill working only ninety-nine percent of the time. But, I mean, ninety-nine percent… that's practically *always*. How the hell did this happen?

If it could happen to anyone, it would happen to you.

Just one more damn mistake. God, even when I'm *trying* to be responsible, I still can't manage to keep my life sorted out. It's so damn discouraging.

I'm going out of my mind being here without Cas. I'm waiting anxiously for him to call me, but I'm dreading it, too. Because once he does, he's going to come back here, and I'm going to have to tell him everything. I've screwed this up too many times. I can't keep all of this from him for one second longer.

A thump at the door jars me from my reverie. I almost go to open it, thinking it's Cal. But then I realize he definitely would have texted or called me to tell me he was coming back.

Another pound, then banging. My heart starts to race as I consider that whoever is behind the door isn't here for a social call.

And then, as I stare in horror, I see the knob jiggle and hear the sound of a key turning.

Without thinking, I fly to the closet and grab for the high cubbyhole, my hand flailing around until it finds the gun. I had completely forgotten about moving it, and I'm almost dizzy with relief that it's still there. I try to shout, to warn whoever is coming in to stop, but my voice leaves me at the critical moment and all that comes out is a harsh wheeze of terror.

When the door opens, I'm pointing the gun straight at the opening, trying not to shake uncontrollably.

It's Charlie Hurt. His face is bloated and bandaged, bits of dried blood under an obviously broken nose. He looks absolutely horrific. Our eyes meet, and for a moment, I'm so shocked at his appearance I almost start to lower the gun.

Then he laughs.

It's a chilling sound. His broken nose means his breathing is altered, and the laugh is guttural, deep and almost animal.

His face — what I can see of it — twists into an ugly leer. "You gotta be fucking kidding me," he snarls.

"Get out of my house, Charlie," I shout. "My dad is not going to like that you broke in here and scared me half to death."

"You stupid bitch." His eyes narrowing in disgust. "You have no fucking idea what you're talking about. It ain't your dad who sent me. Your dad's got a price on his head, did you know that?" He snarls and spits pink on the ground. "He's, fucked, little lady. When the people I work for get their hands on him, he's done."

My heart starts to race as I try to make sense of what he's saying. Charlie's not working for my dad? He's working for someone who's looking for my dad — someone who wants to hurt him — to kill him!

A sob of terror rises in my throat, but I fight to swallow it down. If they're looking for my father, then why is Charlie here? "I don't know where my dad is," I stammer. "He's not here! Please leave!" My voice starts to rise. "Please!"

Charlie chuckles and shakes his head, as if he's amazed at how stupid I am.

"I know he's not here, you dumb cunt," he spits out. "He's not the one I'm here for." He takes a heavy step toward me.

"Stay back!" I cry. Blood rushes in my ears as I tell myself that I may really have to do this. I thought seeing the gun would stop him in his tracks, but it's obvious that he doesn't believe for a second that I'll shoot him.

Or else, I think crazily, *he doesn't care.*

Hurt takes another step toward me. I resist the urge to shriek, and level the gun at him, crouching slightly into a shooting stance.

"I mean it, Charlie!" I tell him. My voice comes out high and reedy. "I'm prepared to shoot you."

"You have no idea what you've gotten yourself into," Charlie Hurt rasps. "You can't fuckin' scare me. You've got nothing on how scary the people who sent me are."

I open my mouth to respond, but just then a sound to my left stops me.

"Mommy?" Noah says in a small, questioning voice. "Why are you yelling?" He looks from me to Hurt, confusion clear on his face.

"Honey, you go back in the bedroom," I say in a quavering voice. "Okay, baby?"

Hurt cuts me off. "No. You stay, kid." Noah stops in his tracks, not knowing who to obey.

"Noah!" I say more sharply. "Go to my bedroom and lock the door!"

Hurt barks, "Noah! If you want your mom to be okay, you'll stay right here." He turns to me with a terrible, inhuman gleam in his eye. "This is even better. I was going to bring the Spiders Abe's daughter for leverage. But Abe's grandson is even better."

No! An almost blinding flash of terror threatens to knock me off my feet. But it's followed by a wave of pure, maternal rage. *I have to protect Noah. I have to protect this baby. I have to keep us safe for Cas.*

"Don't touch him!" I yell at the top of my lungs. "Don't you dare touch him!"

Hurt lurches forward toward Noah and I know what's going to happen next. "Noah, RUN!" I scream. His little pajama'ed feet squeak as he darts off down the hallway. *Oh, God, don't let Noah see this,* I pray.

The gun goes off. The noise is deafening.

But the sight of what I've done is even worse.

Chapter 33

CAS

When I pull up to the address Angel sent me, every nerve ending is on high alert. I've got my piece tucked into the back of my waistband, and I'm scanning the terrain for any sign of danger.

A couple of the brothers are already here, judging from the bikes parked out front, but I don't see Angel's yet. As I pull up next to the others and stop the bike, I realize with a shock of recognition where I am.

This is Abe Abbott's house.

And the front door's wide open.

As I walk cautiously toward the place, I see it's been broken into. A couple of the small front windows next to the door are smashed in. When I walk through the front doorway,

I see the place has been tossed. Inside, Rock is standing in the living room with Hawk and Skid.

"Looks like a home invasion," Rock says dismissively when he sees I've arrived.

"Jesus," I swear. Tanner Springs doesn't normally see this kind of shit. Especially not at the mayor's house. "Does Abe know about this yet?"

"Abe's gone."

"What do you mean, gone?" I ask. "Like, left? Or like disappeared?"

Rock shrugs. "Dunno. He's AWOL. I haven't talked to him."

Something feels off to me. Rock and Abe aren't exactly best buddies, but they've been business associates for years. The number of deals they've done under the table with each other alone ought to make Rock more concerned about him than he seems to be. I'm not expecting Rock to shed any tears here, exactly, but his indifference makes me suddenly sure something bigger's going on that I don't know about.

A few of the other brothers arrive as we're talking, and wander into the front room with us. "Where's Angel?" I ask.

"He's coming. I sent him on a run up north this morning. He should be back here pretty soon." Rock turns away from me and addresses the others. "Why don't you men go upstairs and look around. See what you can see. Grab anything interesting and report back. We're gonna want to get this place cleaned up before the cops show."

Fucking A. So we're cleaning up evidence. *Goddamn it.* My mind goes immediately to Jenna. Her dad is out there somewhere, and it's looking like he's in danger. And Rock's not telling me something.

"How did you find out about this?" I ask him as we watch the brothers walk upstairs.

"Anonymous tip," he tells me, his tone short. "A friend of the club."

I can tell just by the way he says it he's not about to tell me who the 'friend' is.

I can't figure out what to do. It's like I'm paralyzed, and it's driving me crazy. I *need* to know what's happening, but Rock's a closed book, and I know better than to push him on it. I want to call Jenna, but I can't until I at least have some information for her. And I have to talk to Angel, most of all, but he's not here yet, and until he shows, there's no way I'm gonna be able to get enough pieces of this puzzle to put it together.

About fifteen minutes later, Angel finally pulls up outside. I'm about to go out and meet him when my phone buzzes. It's Jenna. I almost shut it off, not wanting to talk to her until I have more information. But then the hairs on the back of my neck begin to prickle: Jenna wouldn't be calling me right now unless something important was up.

I press answer and step out into the hallway. "Hey."

"Cas!" Jenna's voice is frantic on the other end of the line. "Oh my God, Cas. Something's happened. I need help."

Shit. "Okay, okay. Calm down. Tell me what's wrong."

I listen in disbelief and mounting rage as Jenna tells me her asshole landlord broke into her place when she and Noah were there.

"He had his key," she says breathlessly, her voice high and strained. "He opened the door before I could do anything to stop him. His nose was broken, and his face was all bandaged up." Jenna stops talking for a second, and I can hear her take a few deep breaths. I can tell she's working hard to stay calm. "He… he told me that my dad has a price on his head, Cas! He said he was going to bring me to the Iron Spiders for leverage… but then Noah…" Her voice breaks, and it takes all the control I have to wait for her to continue. Finally she calms down enough to keep going. "Then Noah came out, and he said he was going to take Noah instead!" Jenna starts to cry. "He started to go toward Noah, and… I shot him… Cas, he's dead! He's here, lying out there on the living room floor. I don't know what to do!"

Holy shit.

The Iron Spiders. They're involved in this. Some of the missing pieces appear and try to assemble themselves in my mind. The Spiders were the ones behind Charlie Hurt being so scared he was willing to risk anything not to give me their names.

But Hurt was working for Jenna's dad, too. Wasn't he?

Or were the bugs in Jenna's apartment the Spiders' work, too?

Jesus. This is all much bigger than I could have realized. I think back to what Hurt said when I tried to get information out of him.

"You think it's Abe I'm scared of? It's not Abe, man. There's nothing you can do to me that's as bad as what they'll do if I tell you. Nothing."

On the other end of the line, Jenna continues to sob. "Okay, baby," I soothe her. "It's gonna be okay. Trust me, okay? Jen?"

"Okay," she says in a small, trembling voice.

I try to think. "Tell me, has anyone downstairs at the tattoo parlor come up to investigate the noise?"

"No," she whispers. "I think they must be closed."

I breathe a sigh of relief. The guys at Rebel Ink are geniuses as artists, but they're shitty businessmen. This is the first time I've ever been glad they have a tendency to close whenever the mood hits them.

"Okay, Jen, look baby, hold tight," I tell her. "I'll be there really soon, with the MC. Just keep Noah away from the body and don't answer the door until I text you it's me."

I get her to agree, and then I hang up the phone. For a second I feel guilty that I didn't tell her about her dad, but I don't want to risk pushing her over the edge. Not until I can be there to catch her if she falls.

Angel is just walking in as I slide the phone back into my pocket.

"Brother," I greet him, giving him a quick embrace and a clap on the back.

"What the fuck is going on here?" he asks, looking around at the devastation.

"Break-in," I tell him. "Your dad's gone."

"Who has him?" Angel demands. Rock walks up in time to hear the question.

"Hard to say," he answers evenly.

"Angel," I say, "I think this might have been the Iron Spiders."

"The Spiders?" Angel repeats, not comprehending. Then his face changes. "Was he in business with them?"

I nod. "I think so."

I tell him what I know, piecing what I can together and trying to guess at the rest. When I'm finished, Angel is looking at me in amazement.

"God *damn*," he says, looking at Rock. "Did you know this?"

Rock snorts. "No, I didn't fucking know it," he spits. "Not for sure. Not until now. Goddamn piece of shit is lucky to be alive."

If he is alive, I think.

"Fuck. We have to find him," Angel declares, shaking his head.

"No," Rock barks. "Abe had this coming. Whatever happens to him now is on his own head."

"Rock. He's my fucking father." Angel looks him hard in the eye. "Traitor or not. I have to at least try."

"Yeah," Rock growls, his jaw pulsing. "Which is the only reason why I'm not sending out the whole MC to find him and fucking kill him right now."

He turns away and stomps off upstairs, leaving the two of us here alone.

"I have to go try and find him, Ghost," Angel says grimly, turning to me. "He's a piece of shit, but he's my father. And Jenna's."

Fuck! I have to tell him about Jenna. "I know," I reply. "Look, there's something else you need to know. Jenna just called me. Her landlord, Charlie Hurt — turns out he was on the take for the Spiders, and maybe your dad. He just broke into Jenna's place and tried to take her and Noah. Jenna shot him."

"Jesus fuck!" His eyes narrow in anger. "Is she okay?"

"She is, but *he's* not. She killed him." I let out a breath. "You know I'd come with you to look for your dad, but I've got to get to Jenna first, Angel. She's freaking out. Fucking Hurt's lying in a pool of blood on her living room floor."

"No, you're right." He's shaking his head. "You go to her. Take some brothers with you. We don't know for sure whether the Spiders have my dad yet. I'm gonna go on the assumption he got away in time. Anyway, if he didn't..." He trails off, looking around the wrecked house.

I nod. "Yeah. I know."

If he didn't, we're probably too late.

Chapter 34

CAS

With Rock's okay, I take five of the men with me to Jenna's place, including two in one of the club's vans. We pull up just as the sun is setting.

Which is gonna be useful for the next couple of hours.

I text Jenna as we're climbing the stairs and she opens the door, white-faced and frightened. "Noah's in my bedroom," she whispers when she lets us in.

"How is he?" I murmur, drawing her into my arms. For a moment, she collapses against me, and I realize how tightly she must have been holding her emotions in, waiting for me to get there.

"I think he's okay," she says shakily. "He didn't see… what I did." Her breath hitches and she pushes down a sob.

"I made him run to the bedroom and close the door. He was scared of the loud noise, and I just told him I slammed the front door really hard." She manages a wobbly laugh. "I guess I should be glad he's still young enough to believe me when I tell him unbelievable things."

"Sshhh," I whisper, grazing my lips across her forehead. "Let's go check in on him, okay?" I lead her through the living room, past the brothers who are already starting to work on cleanup. Jenna averts her eyes and shudders slightly as we pass.

Pushing open the door to her bedroom, I wait for her to walk through it and then close it behind us. Inside, Noah is sitting in the middle of the bed, a small, frightened-looking animal, clutching Chip-Chip.

I sit down on the bed and give him a smile. "Hey, buddy," I say softly.

Noah doesn't say a word. He just crawls over and climbs into my lap.

I look over at Jenna and raise my eyebrows. Her expression softens as she watches us. I put an arm around Noah and slide myself back against the headboard. He leans into my chest and closes his eyes.

"Wow," I mouth at Jenna.

Jenna slides up beside me and takes my hand. The three of us stay like that for a few minutes, not speaking. Soon, I hear and feel Noah's breathing even out. He's fallen asleep. I look over at Jenna, and I see she's realized it, too.

"He's… had a pretty rough day," she murmurs.

"Sounds like he's not the only one."

She laughs softly and nods. "Yeah, even for me, this is not going to go down as one of my better days." She glances over in the direction of the living room. "What's going to happen to… him?" she asks, a note of fear in her voice.

"The men will take care of the body," I tell her.

"What about the police?" Her lip trembles. "I don't want to go to jail, Cas."

"Sshhh, Jenna," I say, tightening my arm around her. "It's gonna be okay. The club's got… well, let's just say the club's got a reasonably good relationship with law enforcement around here. Sometimes they can be encouraged to look the other way." I think for a moment. "And as far as I can tell, Hurt isn't someone who had a lot of relatives who'll be asking around about what happened."

"Are you sure?" she whispers.

I nod and kiss the top of her head. "Don't worry, babe. It's gonna be alright."

We sit like that, quietly, for a couple of minutes. Jenna clings to me tightly, and I wait until I can feel the tension in her body begin to ebb out of her. Finally, when I feel like I can't put it off anymore, I take a deep breath.

"Jenna, I need to tell you something," I begin. "I probably should have told you over the phone, but I wanted to do it in person. It's about your dad."

I tell her about the text I got from Angel, and what I found when I got to the address he sent me. "I didn't recognize the address at first, until I got to the house. The place was trashed, and your dad is gone."

"Oh, my God," she breathes. "Do you think he's been kidnapped?"

"I don't know," I admit. "Either that, or he realized that the Spiders were coming for him and got out in time." I look over at her stricken face, and my chest constricts. "Angel's out looking for him," I add quickly. "If he's out there to be found, your brother will find him."

What I don't say — and what I sure as hell hope she doesn't ask me — is what will happen to him if the Spiders find him first.

Jenna begins to cry softly. I don't know what else to do but hold her, and let her. The sun goes down, and it grows dark, until the only light in the little room is the tiny lamp on the bedside table. Time passes, and I hear the brothers moving around in the other room. Finally, the front door closes for the final time. They're gone, and we're alone.

I must fall asleep, because when I wake up the three of us are still lying on the bed. Noah's curled up into a little ball, his thumb having drifted into his mouth at some point. I stand and pick him up, then carry him to his room and tuck him in.

When I come back, Jenna's awake. She gives me a small smile as I kick off my shoes and climb back into bed with her. "Hey, there," I murmur, kissing her softly.

"How's Noah?" she asks, glancing toward the door.

"He's good. Out to the world." I chuckle. "Oh, to be young again, and be able to sleep like that."

"He really seemed to need you to comfort him," she says slowly. There's a strange expression on her face.

"Sometimes a boy needs a man to look up to, I guess. It must be rough on Noah sometimes, not having a dad." I glance at her. "Not that you're not doing a great job with him, Jenna. You're a terrific mom." I stop for a moment, considering my words. "Besides," I continue. "Now that you're my old lady, Noah's my responsibility, too. We're a family. Right?"

Jenna's reaction isn't at all what I'm expecting. Her lip trembles, and then suddenly she bursts into tears.

"Hey, hey!" I say, alarmed. I take her face in my hand and turn it to mine. "Jesus, Jenna, I'm sorry!" I guess the stress of the day must still have a hold on her. Not surprising; it's not every day you have to kill a man in your own living room.

"No, no," she sobs. "It's... it's not you..." She shakes her head furiously. "Cas, oh my God, I'm such a fool. I'm so sorry..."

"Jenna, calm down, baby. It's okay," I soothe. "Tell me what's wrong." There's a strange germ of an idea forming in my head, but I force myself not to jump to conclusions. "Come on, Jen," I urge her, pulling her back into my arms. "Talk."

Finally, she manages to calm herself enough to speak. Jenna pulls herself upright and draws away from me, until she's facing me and we're no longer touching. She pulls her legs in tight and hugs them against her chest.

"Cas," she whispers as she looks at me. Tears continue to stream down her face. "You're Noah's father." She takes in a shuddering breath and squeezes her eyes shut. "I should have told you. I should have told you so long ago... I'm so sorry."

It feels a little like I've been punched. Of all the things she could have been preparing to say, this one leaves me speechless. For a moment, it's like the words can't quite penetrate my brain.

Holy hell.

Noah's *mine*? I've been a father for four fucking years, and I never knew it?

In a daze, my mind goes back to that summer when Jenna and I were first together. All that time since, all the months and years after she left, I've been just living my life, with no idea I had a kid. And Jenna's been doing it all on her own. The pregnancy, the birth, raising him… without anyone to help her.

Why did she never tell me?

Damn Jenna and her pride. As long as I've known her, she has the toughest time accepting any help from anybody. Another girl would have come home and leaned on her family during the pregnancy, and the birth. Not Jenna, though. My chest aches a little bit to think about how alone she must have felt through all of it.

But why not me? Why didn't she ask the father of her child to help her?

Because she didn't want to push you into it. The answer comes to me immediately. *Jenna would never want to think you were with her just because there was a baby on the way. She'd rather be alone than be a charity case.*

I haven't said a word since she told me. I've just been sitting here silent. I look over at Jenna to see she's opened her eyes again. She's looking down and away from me. Her jaw is tense, her posture rigid. I realize she thinks I'm angry with her. And to be honest, I am.

But the anger I feel isn't anything compared to the other things welling up inside me.

Joy. Pride. Love.

A little fear, if I'm honest.

Holy fuck. I'm a father.

I have a *son*.

And Jenna Abbott, the one woman who ever made me slow down and think about settling down, is his mother.

"Why didn't you tell me?" I ask, even though I sort of know the answer. I need her to tell me why.

She looks down at her hands. "Because we told ourselves it was a mistake back then. I never wanted Noah to think he was a mistake. I never wanted anyone to think he was a mistake."

Jenna takes a deep breath and forces herself to meet my gaze. She puts a careful hand on her stomach.

"And this isn't a mistake either."

Chapter 35

JENNA

I know he's going to be furious.

I've left it too long; it's too much to handle all at once. Finding out that you're a father to not just one child, but two, in the span of thirty seconds is enough to make any man run screaming.

I know Cas loves me. I do. But I have no right to expect him to take all of this on. I *won't* saddle him with this, though. I won't make my children grow up with a father who doesn't want them.

Cas's face turns dark, and stormy, and I take a deep breath and wait for him to explode.

"Jenna," he says, fiercely but with a gentleness that takes me by surprise. "You were never a mistake. Never."

I don't know what to say to that, so I hang my head and don't respond for a moment. My heart leaps with hope at the fact that he didn't immediately get up and leave, but I force myself to admit that this doesn't mean anything. I'm not going to beg and plead with him to stay with me. I'm just going to tell him the truth — *finally* tell him the whole truth — and whatever he decides to do with it, I'm just going to have to accept.

"I know I should have told you," I murmur. "I've been trying so hard to figure out how to explain. And every day, it got harder instead of easier to tell you." I put my hands to my still-flat stomach. "And now this."

My eyes meet his. "I just found out, Cas. Just a few hours ago. I took the test while I was waiting for you to come back." I raise my head. "And this time, at least, I knew I couldn't make the same mistake with you I made last time. I knew I needed to tell you everything, right away. But you're not under any obligation here," I continue, my jaw setting with determination. "I'm not asking for anything, Cas. I just wanted to do right by you this time. That's all."

"Jenna…" He reaches forward and grabs me by the shoulders. "Do you really think I'd leave you alone in this?"

"I *know* you'd do the right thing," I reply sadly. "But that's just it. I don't want it to be like that. I don't want my children's father to feel obligated to us. I don't want a… a partner who's only with me because he thinks he has to be. I'd rather that these children have only one parent who really wants them, than have to suffer through having two but know one of them is only going through the motions."

"Jenna, stop it!" Cas growls, cutting me off. "Remember what I said to you before? Now that you're my old lady, Noah's my responsibility, too. We're a family. That was true even before I knew this." His hand goes to my tummy. "Now it's even more true." His eyes grow dark again. "So don't fucking push me away."

"You're mad," I murmur.

"Hell yes, I'm mad!" he half-shouts, then his voice drops as he remembers Noah's sleeping next door. "But not for the reason you think." He raises his hands in a frustrated gesture. "I'm mad because you seem determined to believe I don't want these kids. You're hell-bent on believing that I'll be making this huge sacrifice by staying with you. Jenna, *Jesus*." His voice breaks a little. "You keep saying you don't want these kids to feel like mistakes. Why are you letting *yourself* feel like a mistake?" He takes my head in both of his hands, making me look at his earnest, serious face. "You're the best fucking mistake I ever made, Jenna Abbott," he says, his voice husky. "So stop pushing me away and let me love you."

This time, he doesn't wait for an answer. He brings his mouth down on mine, in a kiss that's sweet and soft, but with an intensity behind it that's unmistakable. Our tongues dance, and in that moment I know he's telling me the truth: that he wants me. That he wants *this*.

A life together. Us. With our children.

For the first time maybe ever, a bunch of puzzle pieces seem to fly together in my mind. All my life, all the mistakes I've made, seem to reassemble themselves into a picture of wholeness, of perfection.

What if all the mistakes I've ever made weren't mistakes at all? What if they were just all the pieces that needed to happen to get me here? Where I was supposed to be all along?

"Oh, wow," I breathe as Cas's lips leave mine.

"What?" His mouth begins to burn a path down my neck. "I thought you were used to my massive size by now."

In spite of myself, I snort. "That's not what I was wowing about."

"What, then?"

His hand slips under my shirt, his thumb grazing my already-taut nipple. I gasp with pleasure. "Tell you later…" I manage to croak out as my hands reach to fist in his hair.

He removes my shirt and bra and his hands cover my breasts, cupping one and bringing it to his mouth. The instant his tongue swirls around the hard bud, I'm overcome by lust, a bolt of electricity jolting straight to my core. He teases me, chuckling low in his throat as I whimper and squirm at his touch. His mouth remains locked on my nipple, but his hands leave my breasts to open the button on my jeans. He slides them over my hips, and I do everything I can to help him, but I can barely think straight, already anticipating what I know he's about to do to me.

Cas slides a hand between my legs, and they fall open for him of their own accord. "You're so fucking wet," he groans against my skin. "God damn it, I love how fucking wet you get for me."

"I want you inside me," I whisper. "I need it. I can't wait."

I don't need to beg him. He throws off his clothes and is kneeling next to me in a heartbeat. The beauty of his hard cock never ceases to amaze me. I reach out and wrap my hand around the shaft, loving the hot velvet of his skin. He takes in a sharp breath and watches me, thrusting into my palm just slightly with every stroke.

"Fuck me, Cas," I ask him simply.

He moves between my legs, sliding his large head against my wet folds. I throw back my head and moan, the anticipation already driving me crazy. I close my eyes and wait for him to enter me, but for a second he hesitates. I open my eyes to see him frowning above me.

"Is it okay to do this?" he asks.

"What, you mean because I'm pregnant?" I giggle. "Considering that the baby's about the size of a pin head, I think we'll be okay. Plus, the good news is, I'm already pregnant, so no need for birth control."

"Good points all," he growls, grabbing my hips and pulling me closer to him.

Cas slowly slides his shaft into my waiting channel, and I let out a low moan as he fills me up. I clutch at the sheets, my back already arching. He begins to move inside me. "Oh, God," I gasp. "That's so good. So, so good."

Cas's rhythm starts to speed up. "It's pretty hot fucking a pregnant chick," he rasps.

I grip his strong thighs, pulling him into me, wrapping my legs around him. "More. Harder," I urge. The slide of his cock, slick from my juices, is delicious and hot against my pussy. I arch my hips, adjusting the angle just tiny amounts to increase the pleasure as he continues to slam into me. God, I had no idea how good it felt to be fucked *hard* until I met Cas. It's never too much. I'll never get enough of him.

My breath comes shorter and harder as he thrusts, my need becoming more urgent. Already I'm so close, I know it's just a matter of seconds before I lose control. Cas grabs my hips and pulls me hard against him. "God, I love fucking you, Jenna. I can't get enough. Come with me, baby, come now!"

My pussy swells tight around his cock and I come hard, my muscles spasming as he releases deep inside me again and again. It's just as good as it always is with him. But this time it's better.

This time, I know it's forever.

Chapter 36

CAS

The deepest, best sleep of my entire fucking life is interrupted at three a.m. by the sound of my phone vibrating next to my head.

Groaning, I carefully detach myself from Jenna and lean over to grab the thing from the nightstand. Angel's name flashes on the illuminated screen. I turn away from Jenna's sleeping form and press the button to answer.

"Hey," I mutter quietly into it, hoping I won't wake Jenna.

"Hey," Angel responds. "I need to talk to you. Need to give you a heads up."

"You find him?" I ask.

"Yeah." Angel sounds tired, and pissed, and stressed. "I had a hunch about where he might have gone to hide out. Turns out I was right. Abe's been fucking double-dealing all along. With the Lords, and with the Iron Spiders, too. You know that deal he was trying to close with Rock and our club for the loan? Part of the money was gonna go to pay off a debt he already owed to the Spiders." Angel's voice turns angrier. "And when the club voted against the loan, Dad went to the Spiders and offered to try to sell them information on us as another way to pay them back."

"Son of a bitch," I swear. I swing my feet to the floor and sit up.

"No shit," Angel agrees.

"So, is that why Hurt bugged Jenna's place?"

"Yeah." Angel laughs, a short, dry sound. "I guess Hurt told Dad about you and Jenna, and Dad was fucking desperate enough to think maybe he could get some intel on us through listening in on you."

"What was Hurt's angle, you think?" I ask him.

"Dunno." I hear Angel light up a smoke on the other end. "Dad freaked out when I told him Hurt said he was working for the Spiders. Maybe Hurt figured he could cash in by selling Dad out or something." He takes a long drag and blows it out. "Not sure we'll ever know."

"Rock's gonna want Abe's head for this, if he finds out," I say carefully.

"I know." There's a sound in the background that might be a voice. "If the Spiders don't get to him first, that is. The only way to keep him safe now is to get him out of town. Maybe out of state."

"Where are you at right now?"

"It's best you don't know," he says, his voice flat. "I probably shouldn't even tell you this much. But I'd have to tell Jenna. And you're family, now."

It's true. Jenna's family is mine now. Just as much as the club's my family.

"What are you gonna say to Rock?" I murmur.

Angel sighs. "The only thing I can tell him. That I went out looking for Abe and couldn't find him. That I assume the Spiders got him. That I'm pretty sure he's dead."

"Jesus. That's a pretty serious, uh, lifestyle change for your dad," I say. "He prepared for this?"

"It's better than being dead," Angel says bitterly. "He says he's got someplace he can go. Some assets he can draw on. I think maybe he's been preparing for something like this. I ain't gonna ask him where he's off to, though."

I nod to the phone. "Probably best."

"Thing is," Angel continues, "The three of us are gonna have to stick to that story. You, me, and Jenna." He pauses. "I know that's a tall order, brother. Asking you to keep a secret from the club."

It *is* a tall order. Rock expects absolute loyalty from everyone in the Lords of Carnage. And that's as it should be. You don't survive as an outlaw MC unless you have that from every one of your members. That's why it takes so long to prospect. That's why the vote for someone to get patched in has to be unanimous. Every single member of the club has to be confident that anyone new would fight and die for us all.

And I would. I'd lay down my life for any one of my brothers. That's a given. They're my family.

But Jenna's my family now, too. As is Angel. And as fucked up as Abe Abbott is, he's my children's grandfather.

I understand the need for vengeance. Club justice is Old Testament shit. An eye for an eye.

But in this case, I'm not going to let Abe Abbott's stupid mistakes hurt everyone around him. I won't let his fuckups hurt my family.

I make my decision.

"You've got my word, brother," I tell Angel.

I hear him exhale. "Okay. Thanks. You'll tell Jenna?"

"I'll tell her," I say.

Next to me, she stirs and opens her eyes. "Tell me what?"

"That her?" Angel asks. "Shit, I don't mind telling you this is gonna take a little getting used to, you and Jenna."

I laughed. "You'll have plenty of time, brother. Talk to ya."

I hang up and gather Jenna into my arms. I tell her it was her brother on the phone. I explain everything that Angel just told me: what her dad's been up to, that Angel's with him now, and that Abe is going to have to disappear. She cries. I hold her.

Later, after she's mostly stopped crying, Jenna tells me about the Abe Abbott she knew. About the father she remembers.

"It's so sad," she says, looking down at her hands. "My dad has made so many shitty choices in the last few years. Ever since my mom died, it's like the only thing he cared about was money and power." She shakes her head in disbelief. "Even to the extent of cutting a deal with the Iron Spiders, apparently. God, I *never* would have guessed he was capable of that."

I understand what she's saying. Angel told me back then that he'd overheard Abe on the phone one day not long after their mom Maria had died in a car accident. Abe was talking to Rock. Apparently, Rock thought Maria's death might have been payback to Abe for striking a deal with the Lords instead of the Spiders for territory. If he really believed that, it's fucking sickening that he'd enter into any kind of deal with the MC that killed his wife.

"My dad was never really the same after my mom died," Jenna continues. It's almost like she's talking to herself. I just listen, and let her say what she needs to say. "I mean, he was always driven, you know? He was always really proud to be a successful and important man in Tanner Springs. But after the accident, he just sort of… *disappeared* as a father." She looks at me. "I think maybe every time he looked at Gabe and me, he just saw an empty space where my mom should have been."

Jenna sighs. "Pretty soon, the only thing that seemed to drive him was making deals and getting reelected." Jenna shifts now, and sinks against my chest. She sounds so tired. "Maybe doing business was the only way he could forget what happened to his wife. To erase that part of his life. To feel like carrying on living actually had some meaning." Her voice cracks, and turns tinged with acid. "I guess he did a pretty good job of forgetting all of it, if he could stand to do business with the Iron Spiders."

Jenna starts crying again, quietly. I don't know what to say, so I don't say anything. She collapses against me, and a wave of protectiveness rears up inside me, so fierce it almost scares me.

I will never, ever let her get hurt again.

"Jenna," I murmur, my voice husky with emotion. "I'm sorry. I'm so sorry you have to go through this."

"It's just," she says in a small voice, "I feel like my whole family is disappearing."

"*I'm* your family," I tell her fiercely. "You're *my* family." I put my hand on her belly, marveling that there's a whole other life in there. One that we created together. "*This* is our family."

"I know," she whispers. She lifts her head to look at me. Her eyes are shining with tears, and with something else, too. "I love you, Cas Watkins."

"I love you, Jenna," I say, feeling the strength in the words, like a prayer. "Forever."

EPILOGUE

JENNA

"Daddy!" Noah cries, running through the brightly-colored autumn leaves. "Carry me!" He reaches up his little arms to Cas, his eyes beseeching.

"Noah, you're six years old! You're a big boy now," I admonish him as we walk along. "You can walk on your own two legs."

"But I'm *tired*!" Noah complains dramatically, as though we've been walking for hours. His eyes go from me to Cas, giving both of us his best forlorn and exhausted look. I roll my eyes, but I'm trying not to laugh. Noah loves his daddy so much, he'll use just about any excuse to get a shoulder ride from him.

Cas looks over at me and winks. "You need a birds-eye view, buddy?" he asks his son.

Noah whoops with excitement as Cas scoops him up in his arms and deposits him high on his broad shoulders. I hang back for a moment and watch as the two of them continue down the long gravel drive. Noah is the spitting image of his father with his deep cocoa-colored eyes and tousle of brown hair. As always, it makes my heart swell to look at the two of them together.

We've been walking for about half a mile now. This road's a little rougher than I remember from when I was a kid. Granted, I haven't been here for years and years. I didn't even know it still existed, frankly, until we got the postcard. I'm glad we decided to park my car further back and decided to walk the rest of the way. I'm not sure we would have had the clearance to make it all the way.

"Good thing we decided not to bring the stroller," Cas remarks, seeming to read my mind.

"No kidding," I agree. My hands instinctively move to the little warm bundle I'm carrying snugly in the wrap against my chest. A little coo of contentment comes from my newborn in response. Adoringly, I kiss the top of her little head and breathe in the intoxicating new baby smell.

"My little baby," I whisper to her. "My sweet little girl."

We've named her Mariana, after my mom, Maria. She was born four months ago, coincidentally in the same birth month as my mother. Looking at my little daughter, I can already see that she's going to have my mom's eyes, and her tangle of blond hair — although Cas insists that Mariana got her hair from me. I let it start growing out and going back to its natural color when I got pregnant, and just last week I managed to trim the last of the darker ends off. I don't know why, but it felt like a liberation to do it. Like I was coming back to myself.

Absently, I reach up and push a strand back behind my ear just as we round the last wooded corner. A tiny house comes into view, one that's seen better days and definitely needs a paint job. I'm not sure if Dad's been hiding out here the whole time, or if he's just come here as a way to see us. The only thing on the postcard was an address. Angel said he'd gotten one, too, but he's coming out here separately.

It's the first time any of us has seen my dad since he had to disappear last year. For a while, I was half-convinced he was dead. But he must at least be somewhere close enough that he knows a little about Angel's and my comings and goings, because the address where he sent the postcard was the right one even though Cas and I moved into a house of our own about six months ago. One big enough for a family of four, and maybe more on the way.

As we approach the little house, a door opens, and an old man steps outside. For a moment, I don't even register him as Abe Abbott, he's changed that much. His hair has gone completely gray, and he's stooped over in a way I don't remember him being. My heart lurches in spite of myself. He seems to have aged ten years in one.

"Wow," Cas murmurs beside me. "He's changed."

Cas takes Noah off his shoulders and sets him down. We each take one of his hands, and the four of us walk up to the front porch of the tiny abode. My father's face breaks into a wide grin.

"Jenna!" he cries, and comes down the steps to greet us. He wraps me in a careful embrace that feels odd, since he rarely hugged me growing up. I hug him back and let him give me a papery kiss on the cheek.

"Hi, Daddy," I say, and smile at him.

"My goodness, look at this!" he says heartily, looking at the baby. "If this isn't a surprise!"

"This is Mariana," I tell him.

Dad's eyes get a little misty as he shoots me a quick glance. He lifts a slightly shaky hand and offers a finger for Mariana to grasp. "Oh, that's something," he half-whispers as her tiny fingers wind around his. "Mariana. Wouldn't your mother have loved to see this?"

"Yes, I think she would have," I smile. A huge, painful lump forms in my throat, and I try my best to swallow around it.

For a few moments, he just stares at Mariana, nodding absently at some thought that only he knows. Then, with a deep breath, he turns and bends down to Noah.

"Well, hello, young man," he says jovially. "Do you remember your grandpa?"

Noah glances up at me uncertainly. "Sort of," he says, his voice full of doubt.

"You remember Grandpa," I tell him. "It's just been a long time, honey." I turn to Dad. "A year's an eternity for a boy that age," I explain. "Don't take it personally."

Dad gives me a sad smile. "I know. It's okay." He straightens, and then turns toward the house. "Well, let's go inside. I can't offer you much to eat or drink, but at least we can sit down and get comfortable."

We follow Dad into the house. Inside, the musty odor that greets us and the film of dust on all the surfaces tell me that he's not actually living here. I didn't notice a car outside, though. A wave of sadness rises up inside me for the thousandth time that I don't — *can't* — know anything about my father's life now. *How lonely he must be,* I think. Even though I know he made his own bed, I can't help but pity him.

We sit down in a tiny living area, on a lumpy couch and some faded chairs, one of which is a rocker. I take out Noah's little tablet and let him settle in a corner with it, then sit down in the rocking chair with Mariana.

"So, Casper," my dad addresses Cas, as though this is a completely normal conversation. "How's life treating you? How's the club?"

"Good," Cas nods. "Fine. Have you talked to Angel at all?"

"I saw him about a week ago," Dad says vaguely. "He tells me the Lords aren't exactly thrilled with the new mayor in town." Dad's eyes flash, a mixture of jealousy and satisfaction that his replacement isn't well liked.

"Yeah," Cas says, his lip curling slightly. "Without you around, Jarred Holloway didn't have any other serious competition." Cas lets out a low snort. "Goddamn, that guy's a tool."

Mayor Holloway has the dubious honor of being almost universally disliked now that he's in office, by both the townspeople and the MC alike. So far, he hasn't done much in town beyond prancing around self-importantly and appointing a bunch of his friends to prominent positions. Personally, I hope it stays that way. He has started making noises about getting "tough on crime," though, maybe hoping that will be a stance that improves his popularity among the people of Tanner Springs.

Dad asks a bunch of questions about the new mayor, clearly enjoying the knowledge that his replacement isn't well-liked. I watch Cas indulge him, and can't suppress a feeling of sadness that my father has been relegated to living his life mostly in the past.

We stay for a couple of hours, until Noah starts to make noise about being hungry. "We probably better go, Dad," I say eventually. I accept Cas's hand as he helps me up from the couch.

He smiles and stands as well. "All right. I understand. It's real good to see you Jenna. You and your little family." He looks at me gently. "You seem happy."

"I am, Dad," I smile, moving into Cas's arms. "I am."

Dad accompanies us out to the front of the house and walks with us a little way down the path. Eventually, he tells us he's going to turn back.

"When will we see you again?" I ask him, offering my cheek for him to kiss it.

"Oh, I don't know," he murmurs vaguely. "I suppose one of these days I'll be back around here and we'll get together again." A flicker of sadness and fatigue flits across his face, in the span of an instant. Then it's gone. "You two take care, now. Cas, good to see you." He sticks out his hand, and Cas takes it.

"You, too, Abe," Cas nods. "Noah, come on! Let's go."

Noah runs down the path toward us, and we walk back the way we came. We bundle the kids into the car and Cas takes the wheel to drive us back to Tanner Springs.

"He seems okay," Cas murmurs to me as he drives. He reaches over and takes my hand in his, squeezing it. "As okay as he can be, anyway."

"Yeah." I squeeze back, torn between sorrow for my dad and thankfulness that he's even alive. I know his mistakes brought him to where he is now. But I also know that maybe, just maybe, if a few things had turned out differently, he and my mom might be sitting on their front porch right now, fussing over their grandkids as the sun sets.

Mistakes can take over our lives, snowballing out of control until they roll over everything else in their path. That's what happened to my dad. I just hope he can find some peace, and that maybe someday, he'll be able to have a life again that makes him happy.

I look over at Cas as he drives our little family home. My love for him feels so overwhelming I almost can't bear it for a moment. Cas senses my eyes on him. He turns to me and flashes me his dazzling, sexy smile — the one I've come to know so well.

"Hey, gorgeous," he winks at me. "You good?"

"I'm better than good," I reply.

"Damn straight you are," he growls, and raises his eyebrows at me.

"Language," I smirk.

"It's okay, Mommy, I'm not listening," Noah calls from the backseat.

Cas and I burst out laughing. From the back, Noah's childish giggle joins with our laughter as we head toward the sunset, Tanner Springs, and home.

BOOKS BY DAPHNE LOVELING

Motorcycle Club Romance
Los Perdidos MC
Fugitives MC
Throttle: A Stepbrother Romance
Rush: A Stone Kings Motorcycle Club Romance
Crash: A Stone Kings Motorcycle Club Romance
Ride: A Stone Kings Motorcycle Club Romance
Stand: A Stone Kings Motorcycle Club Romance

GHOST: Lords of Carnage MC
HAWK: Lords of Carnage MC
BRICK: Lords of Carnage MC
GUNNER: Lords of Carnage MC
THORN: Lords of Carnage MC
BEAST: Lords of Carnage MC
ANGEL: Lords of Carnage MC
HALE: Lords of Carnage MC
Forgiveness: A Lords of Carnage MC Christmas

Dirty Santa (Novella)
IRON WILL: Lords of Carnage Ironwood MC
IRON HEART: Lords of Carnage Ironwood MC

Sports Romance
Getting the Down
Snap Count
Zone Blitz

Paranormal Romance
Untamed Moon

ABOUT THE AUTHOR

Daphne Loveling is a small-town girl who moved to the big city as a young adult in search of adventure. She lives in the American Midwest with her fabulous husband and the two cats who own them.

Someday, she hopes to retire to a sandy beach and continue writing with sand between her toes.

Printed in Great Britain
by Amazon